Do's and Don'ts for Dating a Millionaire
by Tallia Venables

1. Don't invite the millionaire back to your place on first meeting if you want him to take you seriously.

2. Don't try to convince the millionaire that you are not attracted to him. He knows otherwise.

3. Do let him know (even if you have to resort to extreme measures, such as clever disguises) that you are so much more than just the pretty woman he's squiring around town.

4. Do kiss the millionaire as often as possible. After all, you never know how long he'll be in your arms—especially when he discovers you are not who he thinks you are!

5. Don't fall in love with him—unless you're planning on confessing all your (unforgivable) secrets to him....

Dear Reader,

Have you ever had a time when you wished you could be two people at once? You know, so one of you could lead your regular life and the other one could see those same people incognito to find out what they were really like (and what they really thought of you)? In Alexandra Sellers' *Occupation: Millionaire,* heroine Tallia Venables pretty much gets that chance. One of her is gorgeous, the other a bit of a plain Jane. The big surprise is what she finds out about sexy Brad Slinger in the process! You're really going to enjoy this one.

And don't miss Kelly Jamison's *The Bride Was a Rental.* Sam Weller is a confirmed bachelor, but suddenly he needs a phony fiancée—fast! Enter Ginger Marsh, willing to take the job but not quite what Sam had in mind. She's a whole lot more than he expected, not to mention a whole lot…sexier. Playing house has never been this much fun before!

Have a good time with both of this month's books, and don't forget to come back next month for two more delightful tales all about meeting—not to mention marrying!—Mr. Right.

Yours,

Leslie Wainger
Senior Editor and Editorial Coordinator

Please address questions and book requests to:
Silhouette Reader Service
U.S.: 3010 Walden Ave., P.O. Box 1325, Buffalo, NY 14269
Canadian: P.O. Box 609, Fort Erie, Ont. L2A 5X3

ALEXANDRA SELLERS

Occupation:
Millionaire

SILHOUETTE YOURS TRULY™

Published by Silhouette Books

America's Publisher of Contemporary Romance

For Leslie Wainger and Nick Cave—what a team!

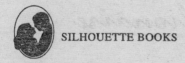 SILHOUETTE BOOKS

ISBN 0-373-52065-4

OCCUPATION: MILLIONAIRE

Copyright © 1998 by Alexandra Sellers

About the Author

Alexandra Sellers has never been either rich or beautiful, but what's imagination for? She is indebted to a Mills & Boon editor for the comment that gave her the title and thus the seed of *Occupation: Millionaire*, but where the idea itself came from, she can't say. "It was one of those stories that just seemed to come on wings. It landed on my shoulder and started singing."

The first person to hear Alexandra's stories is always her editor, Leslie Wainger, "whose ability to point out flaws in structure at that early stage is invaluable. Without her advice I would have written myself into a lot of corners, and that's true again for *Occupation: Millionaire*."

When she has problems with a story in progress, though, "I go to my husband, Nick, tell him what's happened so far and ask him what a man would do in such a situation. It almost always turns out that the reason I'm stuck is that I've misread my own hero. Once I'm straight on his reactions, the story sorts itself out."

Her recent title, *Bride of the Sheikh*, put Alexandra's name on the *USA Today* bestseller list for the first time. Her new book, *Spoken Cat*, a satire "on language, cats and the meaning of life," published in England to a whirl of publicity in 1997, has just been released in North America under the title *How To Speak Cat.*

Books by Alexandra Sellers

Silhouette Yours Truly

A Nice Girl Like You
Not Without a Wife!
Shotgun Wedding
Occupation: Millionaire

Silhouette Intimate Moments

The Real Man #73
The Male Chauvinist #110
The Old Flame #154
The Best of Friends #348
The Man Next Door #406
A Gentleman and a Scholar #539
The Vagabond #579
Dearest Enemy #635
Roughneck #689
Bride of the Sheikh #771
Wife on Demand #833

1

Wanted: Millionaire
Are you rich and want to be richer? Scientist/
inventor whose funding has been withdrawn needs
investment to continue with several promising
projects. Good potential money-spinners.
References. Box 1686, *Vancouver Herald*.

"**M**aybe you'll be luckier this week," Bel said. She
folded the newspaper and tossed it aside to attack her
breakfast egg. "I still think you should run it in the
nationals, though."

Tallia, her sister, nodded silently, chewed and swallowed. "You're right. Next week, if I don't get any response, I'll do that. But I really feel I'd have a better
chance with someone right here in Vancouver. People in
the east—" she was referring to Toronto, not Calcutta
"—already think west coasters have no brains."

There was deep irony in her tone, and Bel grinned.
"And a *beautiful blond* west coaster must have the IQ
of—"

"A garden slug." Tallia sipped her coffee. The two
sisters usually had breakfast together in Bel's apartment,

where the balcony caught the sun in the morning. Tallia's own apartment, one floor up in the same building and on the other side of the corridor, faced west, so they ate their evening meal there together several times a week unless Tallia was working late in the lab or Bel was in the university library. Just lately, there'd been no lab to work in, and shared meals had become a very regular thing.

"So tell me how you got on with Mel Carter," Bel prompted. She knew without being told that the meeting hadn't been a success, but she wanted the details. She'd never laughed so hard in her life as she had since her sister had started running her ad asking for funding.

Tallia gritted gorgeous white teeth at the memory, and wrinkled her perfect nose. "Mel Carter has more arms than the battleship Potemkin. In the end I had to bash him."

Bel opened her eyes. "Wow! How did he react?"

"He said karate was legally a weapon and he'd sue me for assault."

"*Karate?* You don't know karate!" Bel informed her sister unnecessarily. "What the heck did you do to him?"

Tallia shrugged. Her creamy shoulders lifted the torn-off sleeves of the lime green pyjama shirt and her generous breasts pushed against the frayed fabric. "I told him it wasn't karate, just a woman who meant what she said. He was really mad, but so was I."

Bel nodded at the cleavage just showing above the top button of the worn green cotton. "You can't even shrug without starting a symphony," she observed dispassionately. "Poor guy was probably deafened, Tallia."

Bel's sister was a beauty. Even the family had to admit the fact, though it went against the Canadian grain to be so immodest. From the tip of her natural blond head to the toes of her tiny perfect feet, Tallia Venables, twenty-six, didn't have one flaw. She could, and did, model hair, feet, legs, hands, mouth, teeth and eyes for advertisers, as well as her whole body. Her pale hair was thick and soft, and waved gently down to her shoulders. Her wide eyes were an unusual blend of blue and green that made men wax lyrical about tropical seas. Her nose was by Michelangelo. Her mouth was fashionably swollen without any help from injections. Her head floated on her long, elegant neck like a flower on a stem. High, full breasts—which her agent considered just too large for the current fashion but men didn't—flowed into a small, neat waist, and beneath she curved into slim, rounded, fascinating hips. Prize-winning, long, shapely legs, ankles to die for...

Not that Bel was envious. All the Venables were considered good-looking, and it was only next to Tallia that Bel herself could be thought ordinary. And it was hard to envy her fabulous beauty when Tallia had such constant grief because of it.

Something that Bel had only really come to appreciate now that she was at university and living in the same building as Tallia. Now, for the first time since Tallia herself had moved to the city, the two sisters were really close again, the way they had been as children.

It was Tallia's beauty that had taken her away from the family a few years before. An agent had seen her picture and had come to their small town and talked her into giving up her plans to go to university and cashing in on her looks instead. "Your brain will last forever," she had promised Tallia. "If you want to get anywhere on your looks, you have to do it now."

At seventeen, Tallia had fallen for the pitch, and her parents had allowed her to do it, with one proviso. She was not to go any further than Vancouver for two years. If after two years she was managing to earn an income, and if she still hankered after fame and fortune, she could go further. Toronto, Hollywood, and New York would have to wait till Tallia was older than seventeen, whatever the agent threatened about her being past it by age twenty.

It was the smartest thing their parents could have done, because they had as their ally Tallia's brain. After two years of posing and smiling vapidly as Natasha Fox—the alter ego chosen for her by her agent—Tallia had been bored to death. The money was nice, but fame—even the low-key fame of being recognized from advertisements—she found inhibiting. At nineteen Tallia went back to university and her first love, applied science. Her film and modelling career descended into a handy part-time way to support herself without drawing on their parents. And when her sister Bel came to the same university, she could help with her expenses, too. That was the reason she kept it up, even now. And just now she was glad that she had, because the money gave her independence while she decided what to do next.

Tallia was first and foremost an inventor, though, and to the extent that her looks got in the way of that, she found them a hindrance. They were a huge hindrance just at the moment, because she had been artfully manoeuvred out of her university research post by a supervisor who hadn't taken her rejection of his sexual interest with good grace. Now she was faced with a choice—take the job that was offered her in a manufacturing company's R and D department, and work on what they wanted her to work on, or find her own financing, and work on what she wanted to work on.

Thus the ad. But, as Tallia was quickly learning, even greedy multimillionaires who wanted to turn their millions into more millions could be sidetracked—derailed!—by sex. She could describe last night's experience with the wet-mouthed Mel Carter in a way that made Bel laugh, but there was real despair in her voice when she sighed and asked, "Bel, what can I do to convince these people that I really have a brain?"

And Bel said, with the practical good sense that she had inherited from her mother, "It's not that they don't believe you have a brain, Tallia, just that for them sex becomes more important. Maybe you could hide your beauty."

"Hide it, how?" Tallia demanded. "You saw how I was dressed last night! No makeup, hair pulled back, wearing that plain suit…"

Bel nodded absently, thinking. "Marlon Brando," she said.

Tallia squeezed her eyes shut at the unexpectedness of this, then opened them. "What?"

"Cheek puffs. Remember that old film we saw at the Arts Cinema a couple of months ago? He put cheek puffs in, I remember reading that in the brochure. No makeup isn't enough. You have to make yourself ugly. I bet the makeup artist who did your makeup for *Northern Nights* could fix you up."

Tallia stared at her as the idea took hold, with a wide gaze that had been the downfall of many otherwise stalwart males. "Bel!" Then she shook her head. "It wouldn't work. Film's not like real life."

"Sure, come on!" Bel laughed encouragingly. She

was getting into this. "We could turn you into the hunchback of—of—"

She broke off as the unmistakable sound of mail falling through the apartment mail slot caught their ears and Tallia leapt to her feet. "There's the mailman!" she cried unnecessarily.

She ran through the sitting room, tore open the apartment door and ran out into the hall. "Lee!" she called softly. Along the hall the mailman, bending to put something through another slot, turned his head. He smiled. Men always did smile when they looked at Tallia, especially when she was wearing something like the lime green shirt and bare legs.

"Hi, Tallia," he said.

"Lee, have you got anything for me this morning?" she begged.

"Tallia, you know I'm not supposed to do that. There's a directive about it. I could get fired."

"But you know it's me, right? And I know it's me." She walked along the hallway to him. "Natalia Venables. So who's going to want to report you?"

The postman shrugged, as if he'd known it was a losing battle from the beginning. "Hang on a sec," he said, and flipped through the clutch of letters in his hand. "Nothing but bills, Tallia, 'fraid he didn't write again," he grinned, handing her two or three envelopes.

Tallia took them from him with a grateful smile and ran back into Bel's apartment. "Mail!" she carolled to Bel. "Something from the newspaper!"

Bel looked up from her own unsatisfactory bunch of bills. "Quick! Open it!" she commanded. But Tallia didn't need encouraging. She'd already opened the big brown envelope from the *Herald* and was now tearing at the single, slim white business envelope it contained.

"I don't believe it! I don't believe it!" she breathed hoarsely, staring at the signature. Then she looked at the letterhead to be sure.

"Who's it from?" demanded Bel.

Tallia raised her head and took a huge excited breath. "Brad Slinger," she whispered. "Oh, *Bel!*"

"There's no point in my going, Jake," Brad Slinger said. "I can tell you right now I am not going to be investing so much as five cents in any movie. I don't care if he's the next François Truffaut."

"See, that's your problem," his friend and lawyer and sometime investment advisor pointed out reasonably. "Anybody else would have said Steven Spielberg. You're prejudiced against commercial films."

"I'm prejudiced against all films," Brad corrected him gently. "And nothing you or anyone else can say about it is going to make me change my mind."

"Anyway, this is Canadian film we're talking here. It's not an investment, it's a gift. Damon Picton would probably be horrified if a film of his was a commercial success. He'd think it meant he was intellectually stooping."

"Ha."

"Brad, I gotta say it," the lawyer suggested gently. "You're mother-ridden, boy."

His friend frowned, his dark eyebrows snapping together. "How can I be mother-ridden when I've hardly seen my mother since I was three years old?"

Finding it impossible to explain himself, though he knew he was right, Jake abandoned that tack. "Look," he said. "The movies means women. Gorgeous women. You like gorgeous women, Brad. Just come along and take a look at the scenery."

"Gorgeous women, maybe, but not if they're also actresses." Brad flung himself back in his chair. "For—" he began, but just then the phone on his desk rang. "Excuse me," he said instead, and shot out a hand to snap up the receiver. "Yes, Linda."

"Someone named Tallia Venables, Brad. She says she's an inventor and you wrote her a letter asking her to call."

"Her?" he repeated. "Okay, put her through. Brad Slinger," he said, when he heard the click of the connection being made.

"Hi, Mr. Slinger. Did your secretary tell you who I am?" asked a clear, warm voice.

"Tallia Venables. How are you? This is kind of unexpected."

She faltered. "You asked me in your letter to call."

"Yeah. I was expecting Alexander Graham Bell, though."

She laughed a little, though she must be used to that reaction, he thought belatedly. Too used to it, probably. "Well, you've got Alexandra Graham Bell."

They chatted for a moment; Brad found himself liking her. "I don't suppose there's much we can discuss over the phone," he observed after a minute or two.

"I'm afraid I'll need your signature on a confidentiality agreement before we get down to anything serious," she agreed in a businesslike but not unfriendly tone.

"Then suppose we meet? When are you free?"

"I'm free. I haven't got a lab anymore. You say."

"One sec." He put her on hold and pushed his intercom. "Linda, find me a lunch sometime this week," he said, because something in Tallia Venables's voice told him he was going to want this to be friendly and informal.

There was a pause while his personal assistant consulted his calendar. "Well, you can put off Brian Holdiss on Friday. You've been wanting an excuse to do that, anyway," she reminded him dryly.

"Linda, you're a pearl." He went back on line with Tallia Venables. "How's Friday lunch, Ms. Venables?"

"That's just fine," she sang. "Where shall we meet?"

"Give your address to my secretary," he said. "She'll send a car."

"See, now, that's the kind of woman I really admire," he said to Jake when he'd hung up.

"What kind?" Jake demanded incredulously. "You haven't even met her, have you?"

"No, but she's got brains, and I can tell from her voice that she doesn't trade on sex."

"Maybe she doesn't have any to trade on."

"Well, so what if she doesn't?"

Jake just looked at him. "Brad, we have been best friends since the age of six. I have yet to see you with a dog on your arm. In fact, when have I ever seen you with anything less than a real looker?"

"Well, maybe I'll change that. Maybe that's been my problem."

"Problem? You have a problem with women? Since when?"

"Jake, it doesn't take a shrink to see that I can't trust a beautiful woman because my beautiful mother left me and my father when I was three to go to Hollywood. I've been thinking about this lately. Why do you think I'm not married?"

His friend eyed him levelly. "You are not married, Brad, because a: you are only thirty-three and that's too young to be married, and b: you like playing the field. Screwing around, remember? Sowing your wild oats, as my old grandad used to say. Of which you have your fair share, I have to say.''

Brad said stubbornly, "I see now that I'd be more comfortable with a plain woman. I could trust her not to leave me. I might even fall in love with a plain woman.''

"Are you taking leave of your senses? What's this sudden talk of falling in love, and what would you want to do it with an ugly woman for?''

"I didn't say ugly, Jake." He raised a finger. "I didn't say ugly. It's just that faced with this dilemma, I suddenly see things more clearly.''

Jake didn't know whether to laugh or cry. Was his friend serious, or putting him on? Suddenly Jake could see the end of a great lifestyle approaching. He could feel the cool wind of his own mortality breathe across his brow. He shivered. "What dilemma, dammit?''

"See, I've got your frivolous friends in the film business and a lot of beautiful women on the one hand," Brad said, lifting his hand, "and a serious-minded, intelligent, probably plain-looking woman scientist on the other." He lifted the other. "Both of them after funding. And suddenly I see where my real interests lie.''

"Well, I'm glad that's settled. So I'll tell Damon to expect you at the premiere," Jake said, grinning in pretended relief. "You better tell Linda to phone Ms. Venables and cancel.''

Brad looked at him. "See, that's *your* problem, Jake, you can't be serious.''

"That's no problem, Brad," Jake said, just a little frantically. "Come on, just come to the damn premiere. They'll feed us afterwards and put the pitch to us, and what have you lost?" All of a sudden it was a matter of paramount importance to get Brad to the premiere. He began to argue with real feeling.

Finally, with an exasperated sigh, Brad capitulated. "If they want to waste their salmon and champagne on trying to convince me, they're welcome. But I have never invested in film and I don't intend to start now."

Jake stood up. "That's great, Brad." He shot him with a forefinger. "See you Wednesday night." He would call Damon Picton immediately and tell him Brad Slinger was coming and to sic someone gorgeous onto him for the entire evening. If Brad wasn't snapped out of this weird mood, who knew where it would end?

Tallia danced around the apartment after she put the phone down on her call to Brad Slinger. "We're in the money, dum dum de dum dee," she sang. She reached down and dragged Bel up from her chair. "We'll have a brand-new lab de dum dum de doo."

The two girls danced around the room, making up new words to the music. "You're in the money, and ain't it funny, you'll have a secretary and cellphone, too," Bel improvised in a scratchy voice. Then, as they stopped dancing, she asked, "Why are you so sure Brad Slinger is the one?"

Tallia smiled. "Because Brad Slinger owns the Fitness Now chain."

"Really? I thought he was—I don't know, computer stores or something."

"He is computer stores. But he's also Fitness Now."

"So you think he'll like that virtual reality thing?"

"Well, he's supposed to be a man who likes innovation. If I'd thought of it, and if I had the nerve, I should have gone to him right away."

Bel suddenly looked at her watch. "My gosh, I've got

to get to class!'' She ran to the sofa and snatched up her book bag. ''Will you lock up?''

''I'm coming now,'' Tallia said, grabbing her mail.

A few minutes later, as she unlocked the door to her own flat, the phone rang. Tallia tossed her letters down and ran to scoop up the receiver.

''Hi!'' she carolled.

''Natasha?''

''Yeah, hi, Damon!'' she said, recognizing the voice of the film director. ''How's everything?''

''Just wonderful, Natasha. Couldn't be better. Look, are you still coming tomorrow night? I mean, I hope you are, I'm absolutely counting on you.''

''Yes, I'm still coming, Damon. Why?''

''I've got a special project for you. We've got a guy who's up to his eyeballs in money, Natasha, but he never backs films, period. But he's coming to the fund-raiser with a friend. Did you ever meet Jake Drummond, the lawyer guy who did the contracts for me? He's bringing him.''

''And where do I come in?'' Tallia asked resignedly, because she was pretty sure she knew already.

''He likes beautiful women, Natasha.''

''Aw, *Damon!*''

''All you have to do is sit beside him at the dinner and flaunt your assets,'' Damon said pleadingly. ''And tell him how important Talent Films is to Canadian culture. Darling, say you will.''

''Damon—''

''I'm not asking you to sleep with him, Natasha. Just—flirt a little. Get his guard down,'' he pressed. ''And I promise you the part of a thinking woman with no breasts *at all* in my next film. You can wear glasses and be an intellectual and you won't even have to take your clothes off—no, strike that. We'll have one of those revelation scenes—cliché, but oh, so striking, where the ugly duckling is revealed as a creamy-breasted—''

"Digging your grave with your mouth, Damon," Tallia said ruthlessly.

"Darling, I need you to do this thing."

"Yes, I hear you." And then, because he really was a very good director and she knew what it was like to need money for a favourite project, she sighed.

He was quick to hear the capitulation in her tone. "You're wonderful. Look, why don't we make it easy for you? We'll just dress you as Honey, and you can play her all night."

Honey was the part of the American country-and-western singer she had played in the film. Soft, smoky-voiced, sexy. They had given her big hair and what the costumes people had called an "enhanced bra."

Tallia exhaled a breath of relief. "Oh, Damon, do you think I could? Won't he suspect?"

"Natasha, rich businessmen are notoriously stupid about films and acting. Honey is the person he'll be expecting. He'd be disappointed *not* to meet her. I'll ask Marie to bring your wig and other accessories around and help you with your makeup if you like."

"Damon, it'll just be this once, right? I mean, you're not expecting me to have to see him again after Wednesday night?"

"Natasha, that'll be entirely up to you. You might even like him—or his money."

"Ha, ha, Damon."

"As long as you leave some for me. You will do your best for me, won't you?" the director said anxiously.

"I'll tell him you're the next François Truffaut."

It wasn't till she put down the phone that Tallia realized she hadn't asked the rich old goat's name. But she guessed it wasn't important. She'd find out soon enough.

2

_In the film, Natasha Fox played the part of Honey
Childe, a glamorous American country-and-western
singer. Sophisticated if not very intelligent, Honey had
arrived one summer on the small B.C. island home of
the young heroine, and, under her heartbroken gaze, introduced the handsome young man the heroine was in
love with to the joys of sex. Ten years later, hearing of
her suicide, the heroine remembered the anguish of that
summer.

It was a peach of a part, small but pivotal, and it
showed off Natasha Fox to perfection. As the star, on-
stage she was glitzy and polished, but offstage she was
bruised, vulnerable, and searching for her lost innocence.
Her hair tousled and her legs extending forever from the
cut-off jean shorts, she was warm, engaging, sexy and
wistful, and she wrung men's hearts.

She sure got to Brad. He sat through the movie trying
to remind himself he was a fool if he imagined the actress was anything like the role she was playing, but
unable to stop himself responding to her plight—and her
chemistry. The slightly hazy scenes of Honey running
barefoot through tall grass, Honey laughing against the
sun, Honey bending over in those cut-offs to examine a
seashell, Honey licking the young hero all down his

throat and chest...well, it reminded Brad all too clearly of his own sexual awakening. Not that he'd had anyone quite like Honey Childe to bring it out in him, but the urgency was universal at that age, he guessed. And somehow, the onscreen Honey brought it all very sharply back. He kept waiting for the flashbacks. There weren't enough of them.

As the credits rolled, he couldn't stop himself checking the name of the actress who had played Honey. Natasha Fox. If ever there was a name that was made up, Natasha Fox had to be it. Just like the person in the film. *She's an actress*, he reminded himself brutally. *Fake personality, fake hair, fake eyes, fake mouth, fake*...well, not fake legs. Surely they couldn't have faked those.

"I'm leaving," he said to Jake, as the audience stopped applauding at last and the two men got to their feet.

Jake grabbed his arm. "Are you crazy? Didn't you see her? She's perfect, dammit!"

"See who?" Brad demanded mulishly.

"You know damn well who. That's who you're lined up with tonight, Brad! She'll be sitting beside you at the dinner! Don't be a jerk!"

And just to make sure, Jake held on to his arm. It was a deceptively light grip, but it forced him inexorably to the side of the director, standing in the theatre lobby receiving the congratulations of various friends and colleagues in a cosy, exclusive circle. Jake was under no illusions, however. He dragged Brad right up to Damon Picton and introduced him, and immediately Brad had the director's full attention.

"Brad! Good to see you!" exclaimed Damon, abandoning his friends and shaking Brad's hand in the vigorous male way he thought a businessman would feel comfortable with. "Did you enjoy the film?"

"Very good," Brad said shortly. He always felt uncomfortable with people who talked to his money.

"Damon, that was fabulous!" said a very thin, dark, slightly haggard-looking young woman. "I really see why you couldn't cast me as Honey, though I was furious at the time." She kissed his cheek. "Natasha was wonderful in the part. The film is absolute heaven!"

"Thanks, ah—I really appreciate that," said Damon vaguely.

"Melody," supplied the actress, and Brad just stared. Never in his life had he seen anyone so inaptly named. *Melody? Discord* might be more like it.

Damon got rid of the hopeful actress and now had him by the arm, as if fearing that he would escape in the shuffle. "Where the hell's Nash?" Brad heard him mutter to someone beside him. "Anyone seen Natasha?" he demanded in a louder voice.

"Ah'm right heah, Damon, honey," said the voice that seemed to have already imprinted itself into his blood, and Brad looked around at the woman making the crowd part, and it was Honey Childe—from the compelling wide blue-green eyes which he had last seen stretching ten feet wide on the screen, past the incredible half-exposed breasts and that slim waist just asking to be spanned by a man's hands, down to the perfect ankles arching into stiletto-heeled shoes… "What can Ah do for you all?"

Even the voice was the same. Soft, throaty, the drawling Southern U.S. accent like rich fur stroking his spine.

"Natasha, here's someone I'd like you to meet," said Damon.

She smiled, showing perfect teeth. "Why, of course,"

she said, and turned the full wattage on Brad. In spite of himself, his heart leapt. Not just his heart.

"Brad, this is Natasha Fox. You saw her onscreen. Nash, meet Brad Slinger."

Under her makeup, Natasha Fox's face went white. Her eyes and mouth lost all expression. *"B-Brad Slinger?"* she whispered, staggering slightly, and Brad was sure he wasn't imagining the surprise in her tone. Nor the curious fact that she spoke his name with no trace of accent.

Tallia staggered under the shock, and in the stiletto heels she was wearing, that was a near-fatal thing to do. Her foot half turned under her, and if Brad Slinger hadn't been right there, she'd have twisted her ankle for sure. But he was quick and strong, and he caught her around the waist almost before she knew she was falling.

"Thank you," she breathed automatically. Her brain was a fever of activity, trying to work out what to do, how to handle this.

You're Natasha Fox, her brain prompted. *Playing Honey Childe.*

"You all right?" Brad Slinger was asking solicitously. His grip on her was very firm.

"What happened, Nash?" That was Damon. "Did you hurt your ankle?"

"Not at all," she said brightly, back in her Honey Childe mould. "It's only mah shoe, it just caught on the carpet." Damon nodded and clucked sympathetically, his brain whirring. There was something wrong here, that much he knew. Silently he cursed the gods. If Nash and Brad Slinger had a history... Damon turned to Brad again, trying to read his expression. Nothing but the sexual curiosity any straight man would show, meeting Natasha Fox for the first time.

Natasha said to Brad, "Thank y'all for saving me from a fall."

"My pleasure," said Brad, pretty sure that between the two of them he was being conned, but unable to see how. And the more Natasha Fox smiled at him, the harder it was to think. As she gently withdrew from his hold, he drew her hand through his arm and locked it against his side. "You lean on me," he commanded her, and the worst of it was, he meant it.

There was hard muscle under the black tuxedo jacket. Tallia wanted to scream. Why hadn't she asked Damon the rich old goat's name? Why had no one told her that Brad Slinger was such a gorgeous hunk of man? She'd known he was young, she'd read a profile of him in the paper not long ago, part of a series about men and women who'd made their fortune before the age of thirty—that was how she knew he owned Fitness Now—but the picture that had accompanied that article hadn't done him justice at all. It hadn't shown the magnetism in the piercing blue eyes, for a start. Nor the sheer male perfume of his skin...

A few minutes later, Tallia awoke from her confused daze to discover that she was in the back of a limousine with him on the way to the dinner venue. And she still had no idea what to do, how to handle this. She tried to sort out the confusion in her brain by first describing her dilemma. As Natasha Fox playing Honey Childe, she was sworn to do her best to convince Brad Slinger to invest in Damon's next film. On Friday, she had a date as Tallia Venables to meet him and convince him to equip a research lab for her.

And for all she knew he had one investment budget, and only one lucky person was going to get the money. It seemed horribly probable.

Could she possibly come clean now, say, *oh, by the way, by an amazing coincidence I'm also Tallia Venables, the inventor*...Tallia rejected that out of hand. Most men had trouble accepting that she had a brain even when she was dressing down. How could she convince him of anything, dressed as she was? She was even wearing the "enhancement bra" the designer had produced to make sure everyone got the full value of Honey's charms, and then some, by a few cup sizes.

It would be much, much easier to explain on Friday, when she was dressed like her intelligent self, wouldn't it? So, very human, Tallia fell for the temptation to put off an evil moment. She turned to Brad and smiled. "Did y'all like the film?" she asked softly.

"Very much," said Brad instantly. "Especially your part."

She turned away from what she saw in his eyes and smoothed her dress over her knee. "Really?"

"Really," he repeated dryly. "Isn't that why you're here?"

Her gaze flickered back to his face. "Pahn me?"

"Well, you're the sexiest thing in the whole film, aren't you? Has Damon got a part for you in the next one? I bet he has," Brad said feelingly.

"Oh—wh—Ah don't know. Why?"

"Well, then you'd have a real interest in...ah, talking me into an investment, wouldn't you?"

"Ah don't need to have a part in his next film to do that," she said. "Damon's very good. He deserves all the chance he can get."

Brad grinned. "Well, maybe *Northern Nights* will be a commercial success, and he won't need outside backing."

"I hope so." She tilted her head curiously. "Does that

mean you've already made up your mind not to give him any money?''

"Yup," he said shortly.

She blinked. "Why? Y'all just said you liked the film.''

"I liked it all right, but I don't invest in movies."

"What, never?"

"Never ever," he emphasised flatly, in case she thought she might change his mind.

He couldn't understand why that made her smile. "Really? Why? Not enough chance of getting a return on your money?"

"Not exactly." He suddenly realized that he didn't want to be discussing money with her. He wanted to be kissing her. But he supposed she would think it was too soon. Then he thought, *to hell with that.* He leaned towards her, involuntarily inhaling her perfume. It seemed too heavy for her, but there was plenty of extract of civet in it, or whatever it was in perfumes that stimulated male hormones.

He got his mouth about an inch from hers. "I want to kiss you," he said, his voice flat and tight with need.

Tallia caught her breath. It wasn't something she was unused to, this kind of instant reaction from men. What startled her was the shivery response of her own skin and blood. She just didn't get interested in a man as quickly as this. Especially not pushy men. They *always* put her off.

"Ah guess y'all think that's a compliment," she said flatly, fighting for calm.

"I think it's a statement of fact," he said. "Give me your mouth."

"N—no!" she stammered indignantly.

"You want to."

"What makes you so sure?"

He lifted a finger and ran it lightly down the side of her neck without saying a word. She felt her flesh shiver into goosebumps that were certainly visible to him.

She drew sharply away from the touch.

"Ah guess money makes a man pretty confident," she observed dryly.

The shock of it made Brad sit back and take stock. What the hell had got into him? The last person in the world he wanted to get the irresistible hots for was an actress. Especially one who looked like this. If ever he saw a woman who would be off to Hollywood at the first opportunity, Natasha Fox was it. He was only amazed that the opportunity hadn't yet come.

"Sorry," he said harshly. "I thought that was the reaction expected of me."

She eyed him very levelly, and the setting sun just showed him the disbelief in her eyes. "You don't strike me as a man who does what's expected of him very often," she said. "When it suits your purpose, maybe."

Brad laughed involuntarily. Brains, too. The sooner he got away from her, the better. "You're right, the fault is mine alone. I apologize."

It wasn't very far to the dinner venue, and both were grateful to see that the car was already pulling up at the curb. Tallia slipped out and headed into the restaurant in the wake of a small group who had arrived in another car, but if she thought she could avoid Brad for the rest of the night, she was mistaken. Brad might tell himself it would be better for him to let her go, but the sight of her trying to escape brought out the hunter in him and overrode his common sense. As she approached the restaurant door there was a firm pressure against her waist, and Tallia didn't need to look over her shoulder into those brooding blue eyes to know whose hand it was. Her skin had already told her.

In any case, Damon was there, making sure that his plans for Brad and all the other potential financial contributors didn't go awry this evening. Short of walking out, there was no chance for Brad and Natasha to escape his arrangement. Brad couldn't understand why he didn't just walk out. It was the sane thing to do.

Somehow sanity seemed less attractive than the other options.

There were several tables in the privately booked room, each with a sprinkling of the members of the cast and production team among friends and potential investors. Tallia had Brad on one side of her and one of the makeup women on the other side. The makeup woman was under instructions not to draw Natasha's attention from Brad. On Brad's other side a location manager was detailed to keep Brad and Natasha talking.

Neither Brad nor Tallia were aware of these sophisticated arrangements. All they knew was that there seemed to be no way out of talking to each other.

And the champagne flowed. Everybody had at least two glasses before they got anywhere near real food. It was the same champagne that had featured in the film, and had got a credit at the end. The company had been talked into sponsoring the drinks at the dinner, too, according to the little printed cards set discreetly at intervals on the tables.

In the film, the innocent, horny young hero had gone awkwardly into his local liquor store and asked the assistant for help in choosing something really, really sophisticated for his evening with Honey. The assistant had offered this brand, and Honey had, in her dim, sexy way, been duly impressed. And she had giggled and confessed that champagne just did something to her....

Brad was too damn wise in the ways of the world for crap like that, and yet he found himself watching Natasha Fox drink the fizz with bated breath, as if she might lean over and kiss him the way she had kissed the young hero...

"You like this stuff?" he demanded, sotto voce.

"Oh, yes," said Tallia, truthfully. She'd developed a taste for it during the shooting of that scene, which people were saying was so erotic now. She let Honey Childe, or was it Natasha, give him a sexy, sleepy smile, because somehow, as long as it was someone else doing it, flirting with Brad Slinger seemed safe.

"Does something to you, huh?"

"Sometimes."

"Then kiss me," he commanded. His head was bent and angled towards her, and his voice was baldly urgent with need. Tallia caught her breath. But she did not turn away. They were in a cocoon, and it was as if she could not escape from the nearness of him.

"Stop it!" she whispered.

"Kiss me."

"No!"

He swore. He said, "There's a dance floor. Is there going to be dancing?" She knew he wanted to touch her. It was as if he'd asked her to go to bed with him.

"No," she said flatly. Then, "I don't know. If there is, I won't dance with you." She knew that it was a lie even as she said it. He turned and gave her a look that said he'd heard the same thing in her voice.

"How far did Damon Picton ask you to go with me?" he demanded. "What kind of control does he have over you?'' He couldn't believe he was talking like this. He sounded like a madman. But he couldn't stop himself.

"How dare you!" Without knowing what she was doing, Tallia put back one arm to pull out her chair and began to get to her feet.

His strong hand came down on her other wrist. "No," he said. He was angry. He hadn't been made angry by sexual need since he was a teenager. Not even then. Not like this. "If you leave now, I'll get up and walk out."

"You're not going to give him anything anyway. You said so," Tallia whispered furiously, subsiding nevertheless.

He simply ignored that. "You're uscd to this," he said harshly. "You get this reaction from men all the time. Why are you playing coy with me? All I'm doing is declaring you the winner."

Perhaps one of the biggest drawbacks to Tallia's film career was that she truly hated making a scene. She simply could not do what she knew she ought to do now—get up and walk out. On both sides of them, the scene between Brad and herself was being studiously ignored. They were alone.

"You really are the rudest, most arrogant—" words failed her "—I've ever met!" she stormed.

"And I want you," he said. He fixed her with a look. "What do you want to do about it?"

"You're insane!"

He looked at her, letting his eyes talk for him, satisfied when she caught her breath and couldn't look away. He opened his mouth. "Completely," he agreed. He was staring at her mouth. "Do you get injections in your lips?" he asked softly. His intensity was killing her. It was like watching a tiger making up his mind when to eat her.

"Certainly not," she said. At last she was able to look away. Someone was putting the starter in front of her and, relieved at the way the waiter's invasion of their cocoon broke the tension, she picked up a fork.

"You're all natural, are you?"

"You're unlikely to get the chance to be disappointed if Ah'm not," she drawled, suddenly remembering her accent. She couldn't be sure whether it had slipped in those few minutes of insanity or not. But she would take good care it didn't slip again. With a sinking feeling that was close to real despair, she wondered what she could say to him when she met him as Tallia Venables.

"Don't count on it. I'll have one big ally in the enemy camp when it comes to the campaign."

She stared at him. "Who? If y'all think Damon has the—"

He didn't touch her, just looked as if his eyes could sense the texture of her skin. "You," he said softly.

She shivered and bowed her head. She had no armour around him. Lots of men assumed a sexual interest in her, when they had roused nothing in her but resentment and distaste. But this was different. It wasn't masculine self-delusion in Brad Slinger. He knew. He wasn't pumping his ego, he was simply stating a fact. His mouth wasn't loose, either, but firm, almost angry. And his eyes weren't that awful wet she hated to see in men. They glittered like blue ice.

Still, she had to try. "An awful lot of men would like to believe that," she said.

Brad suddenly checked himself. What the hell was he doing, coming on to a beautiful actress like a teenager or...well, he'd seen enough of men talking to women they thought were available. He'd always been disgusted by the attitude. It appalled him that he could be reduced to such a level.

"I'll take a number, then," he said dryly. The punishing note in his voice was directed at himself, not her, but she gasped and threw him an icy look.

"Y'all do that little thing!" she said, and turned resolutely to the makeup artist on her other side.

Not all the makeup artist's attempts could force Natasha to talk to Brad Slinger again after that, and in any case Brad was telling himself that the less he saw of this woman the better off he'd be.

Natasha left the party early, in a taxi. Brad watched her leave from across the room, but made no attempt to stop her. She was exactly the sort of woman he was not going to let himself fall for.

3

Tallia hardly slept, and awoke early to get up and pace the floor, trying to see a way out. At seven-thirty she phoned her sister.

"Mruw?" said Bel drowsily.

"Bel, I'm really sorry to do this to you, but I have a terrible problem," Tallia began apologetically.

"I'll be right up." Bel's voice was suddenly clear. Bel could go from sleepy to dead focussed in two seconds when necessary, and four minutes later she was at Tallia's door.

"What happened?" she demanded, still on the doorstep.

Tallia took a deep breath. "The rich man Natasha Fox was supposed to charm into a donation was Brad Slinger," she told her sister baldly.

Bel's hazel-flecked eyes widened. "Omigosh, really?" She came in and closed the door. "Oh, what a bummer! Is he going to give all his money to the film?"

"He doesn't invest in film. He said so."

"And what did you say? How did you explain about being two people?"

"I didn't. I chickened out."

Bel simply stared at her. "You didn't tell him that

Natasha Fox is Tallia Venables and that you have another date with him tomorrow?''

Tallia lifted her hands as if to protest, then abandoned the gesture. ''No.'' She turned and walked to the kitchen, a gawking Bel following in her wake.

''I can't believe I heard you right! He doesn't know? What are you going to tell him when you see him?''

''That's what you're here for. We have to brainstorm. See, it wasn't just all that simple. He fell for Natasha like a ton of bricks. All strictly physical, of course. When I think of the way I was dressed, I could kick myself!''

''You didn't know,'' Bel pointed out reasonably.

''I doubt if he thinks I've got two thoughts to rub together in my brain. And for sure, for sure he is not going to be able to hear my ideas with sex on his mind. He'll be just all eyes. No brain, no ears. Unless, of course, I say yes.''

''Might you do that?'' Bel asked, astonished.

''No!'' Tallia said fervently. ''Of course not!''

Bel wrinkled her nose as if at a bad odour. ''Ugh! Is he old and horrible?''

Tallia sighed and paused in the making of the coffee. ''No,'' she said. ''He's young and…'' Words failed her, but the shiver of remembered physical excitement that coursed over her skin was not lost on Bel.

''What—he's gorgeous?''

Tallia, her back to Bel, remained silent.

''Did he ask you—Natasha—out for a date?''

''No. He as good as told me we were going to end up in bed, but he didn't get around to offering me dinner or a show first. Then we kind of had a fight and didn't speak again.''

''You had a *fight?* With the millionaire who's your

last best hope for funding? He's a complete stranger, Tallia! How could you get into a fight?''

''You tell me.'' Sinking down into a chair at the kitchen table, and pouring their coffee, Tallia gave her the gist of it. ''So, what can I do now?''

Bel shrugged almost hopelessly. ''Maybe you could put off the appointment a little while.''

''What good would that do?''

''I dunno. You could hope the memory would fade a bit.''

''He'll still take one look at me and know I'm Natasha Fox.''

Bel, in the act of sipping her coffee, suddenly sat up straighter and put her cup down. ''Maybe, maybe not.''

''Come on, Bel, you—''

''No! Remember what we were talking about the other day? About you disguising yourself as ugly? Why don't we just do that little thing?''

Tallia set down her own cup, her eyes fixed intently on her sister. ''Bel, do you think I could? Wouldn't he be able to tell?''

''The trick is to be plain enough that he hardly looks at you, don't you think? The voice is going to be the problem.''

Tallia grinned broadly. ''But, honey, Ah used mah best Honey Childe drawl last naht,'' she whispered breathily. Then she made a face. ''At least, I hope I did.''

Bel cut her morning classes. Ten o'clock found the two girls downtown at the department stores. By late afternoon they had blitzed the shops for everything they needed, then returned home for a dress rehearsal.

''First things first,'' Bel ordered. ''Get in there and

wash your hair." They had decided against a wig for Tallia, because Natasha Fox had worn her big blond wig last night, so her hairline had been disguised and he hadn't seen her ears. They had opted instead for a brunette rinse that would wash out eventually, and made her hair mousy.

"Perfect!" Bel announced, when Tallia had finished with the blow dryer. "That has absolutely zero sex appeal."

Looking in the mirror, Tallia had to agree. The brunette rinse was too weak to change her hair colour dramatically, and had reacted with her natural blond to produce a muddy tone. It looked not very healthy.

"Right! Bra next." It had been Bel's idea that Tallia should flatten her breasts by wrapping them with a large medical bandage. The effect was somewhat lumpy and amorphous.

Tallia had chosen a cheap tan pantsuit in stiff polyester knit, the jacket a size too small and the pants a size too big with a cut that ruined the shape of her hips and thighs, and an awful orange-and-pink polyester blouse with large floppy tie collar that somehow made her neck look thin. Tallia emphasised the effect with a little makeup that shadowed in sinews that did not exist.

Her unusual eyes they disguised with a pair of brown cosmetic contact lenses. Since there had been no time to get them made to prescription, it meant that Tallia would have to wear an old pair of glasses, which she hadn't used since the age of fifteen. The large lenses and heavy frames had been fashionable once, but now they just looked unattractive. The frames were too small for her head, and gave her eyes the appearance of being set slightly too close together.

Bel stood back to survey her critically when this piece

of apparatus went on. "Doesn't exactly make you look like a winner in the brains department, though," she said dubiously.

"Never mind." Tallia was grinning with a kind of illicit excitement. Why had she never thought of this before? Freedom beckoned. She was turning into Plain Jane before her own eyes. It wasn't a difficult matter to change her brow line by penciling in thick, dark eyebrows, and make up badly and with the wrong colours. Browns and oranges simply didn't suit her skin, and made it look unhealthy.

What Bel called the pièce de résistance was the teeth. Tallia had almost forgotten the existence of the fake teeth she had once worn for an orthodontist's Before and After ad. The orthodontist had made them himself. Of thin enamel, they fit over Tallia's own front upper teeth, to make them look crooked and give her an overbite that completely altered the line of her mouth. It had not been false advertising, the agency making the ad had assured Tallia, because orthodontic work would achieve the results the Before and After shots promised. It was just that such work took months or years and they needed the ad now. Since the plate had been made to fit her, she had been allowed to keep it.

When it was all done, the two girls stood in front of the mirror and admired their handiwork. She was not ugly, not by any means. She was just a not-unattractive woman who had no idea how to enhance her good points, or how to dress, but who tried very earnestly to make sure her clothes coordinated. She clearly did not know what hairstyle might suit her or what was in fashion. And she dressed far too old for her age.

"I don't know how you can bear to go out like that," Bel said.

Tallia only grinned delightedly at the reflection, and Bel instantly warned her, "Don't smile like that at him, because it makes you look like yourself in spite of the teeth. Smile with your mouth closed."

"All right," Tallia said. It wouldn't be difficult not to smile at Brad Slinger, she told herself silently.

"And carry yourself like a woman with no sexual confidence. Hunch your shoulders a bit. A walk will give you away as fast as anything."

Tallia nodded and walked up and down the sitting room a few times, getting into character. When the phone rang, she jumped nervously. "I wonder who that is?"

"Nash?" said a troubled voice she instantly recognized as Damon Picton's.

"Hi, Damon," she said awkwardly, wondering if he had called to complain about her behaviour last night.

"Hi, Nash. Look, I just called to say I'm really sorry."

"It's all right," she said. "I survived."

"He's called, then? I tried and tried to call you this morning and warn you, but you weren't answering and your machine wasn't on."

Tallia frowned. "Warn me about what?"

"Brad Slinger got your telephone number out of me last night," the director confessed, all in a rush.

"Aww, *Damon!*" she cried, as a little thrill of fear raced up her spine and burst out over the skin of her shoulders and back.

"I know, I know, I'm sorry."

"Well, I hope you got the promise of some funding for it," she said bitterly.

"No!" he said earnestly. "It wasn't like that, not at all! It was one of those force-of-personality things, you know—honest to God, Nash, I couldn't say no to him. He's just one of those people, you know? I mean, I can see why he's got money. Say you forgive me, darling.''

"Oh, damn!" she muttered helplessly. When she finally got the abject director off the line, she turned to her sister and told her the news. "What am I going to do now? He's bound to want my phone number as Tallia, and he'll notice if I give him the same one...won't he?"

The tag was almost hopeful, as if she thought that Bel might be of the opinion Slinger wouldn't notice, but Bel made a face and said, "If he's calling both of you, sure to."

"Damn that Damon anyway. What did he mean, he couldn't say no?"

Bel raised her eyebrows. "Well, whatever he meant, I'd take it as fair warning, if I were you. Probably you won't find it easy to say no to him, either. You'd better give him my phone number."

"I've got a premonition of complete disaster!" Tallia moaned. "I almost wish he'd phone and cancel!"

Brad Slinger didn't cancel. At noon the next day, after a night of terrible indecision, and a morning of Bel's enthusiasm for the project, Tallia nervously clambered out of the car he had sent for her and went through the doors of a very expensive and exclusive restaurant. The tables were thick with damask and covered in crystal and silver and the waiters were all French, or pretended to be.

"I'm meeting Mr. Slinger," she told the maitre d'.

He nodded elegantly. "Of course, madame." She had dined here several times before, but he did not show any signs of recognition. Tallia knew that it was good business to recognize former clients if at all possible, and breathed a little easier.

The restaurant door opened behind her, and the room seemed to sit up with awareness. Tallia felt the buzz and turned as Brad Slinger walked in. He had a vibrancy and a masculinity that would make anyone notice him, but there was also the unmistakable odour of money, and it was that that made the maitre d' nod in just that way at him. Not the bow that had expressed his superiority to Tallia, but a subtle little inclination of the head and "Mr. Slinger. Always very pleasant to see you, sir. This lady was just asking for you. Your table is this way."

He was dressed quite formally, in a suit and tie. He paused as the maitre d' lifted an arm to usher them to the table. "Ms. Venables," he said, putting out his hand.

The cool friendly formality took her aback, after the hot intensity of their last meeting, but Tallia recovered quickly and put out her hand. All trace of Natasha's dark red nail polish and long, stick-on fingernails had been removed, and all her jewellery. Her flat shoes meant she was two inches shorter than Natasha Fox, and Brad Slinger was looking at her without a trace of predatory interest in his eyes. Suddenly she was confident of the disguise.

"I'm very glad to meet you, Mr. Slinger," she returned, struggling to keep any trace of breathlessness out of her tones. She had lost all her sex appeal, but Brad Slinger still had his. It seemed to affect her breath control, but the breathless voice belonged to Natasha.

They sat down and accepted menus from their host.

"What would you like to drink?" Brad asked, browsing through the wine list.

Men didn't usually talk to her without looking at her.

Tallia blinked with the novelty of the experience. "Um, tomato juice, please," she said to the top of his head.

When their drinks had been brought and their orders taken, Brad seemed to look at her for the first time. He raised his glass to her and drank. Tallia smiled with her mouth closed and drank her tomato juice.

Well, Jake had been right, he observed dispassionately. She didn't trade on sex because she didn't have much to trade on, although he was pretty sure that if she tried a little, she could make more of herself than she was doing right now. He saw that she smiled with her lips closed to hide crooked teeth, but they weren't all that bad. Anyway, she must know that she could get them fixed.

He was pretty expert on the relative cost of female apparel, but the thing she was wearing had him stumped; he didn't think he'd ever seen anything like that. Maybe she'd bought it in a charity shop, or one of those cheap outlets. If he was going to invest money in her, he told himself wryly, he should be glad she wasn't devoted to female fashion. Instead he was aware of irritation. Wasted talent of any kind usually annoyed him, and this woman couldn't have wasted her looks more efficiently if she'd deliberately set out to do it.

He thought about what he'd said to Jake...something about wanting to fall in love with a plain woman. He supposed when he'd said it he had in mind someone dark and thin, interesting looking, not really plain at all. Not someone like this, with her eyes set too close together, mousy hair in an untidy braided chignon like someone's Aunt Mary, a thin neck and muddy skin.

As they chatted, though, he certainly found himself liking her. She was intelligent, which he always liked in people, and it was a funny kind of relief to be with a woman who wasn't trying to attract him physically. She talked to him very straight. He liked that, even though he was honest enough to admit to himself that the manipulative stuff—like Natasha Fox on the night of the premiere, he remembered with a pang of lust—really got to him. Everything about her had been fake, he guessed, except that she, too, had seemed pretty smart, and she could hardly have faked that—and it had all gone straight to his hormones.

Absently he wondered if he could make up his mind to fall in love with someone like Tallia Venables and then do it. He wondered if he could make up his mind to suppress his hots for Natasha Fox and do that. The Natasha Fox kind of woman was fine for what Jake archaically called sowing his wild oats, but he knew from experience that the man who married a woman like that was a fool.

Brad frowned at his own thoughts. It wasn't like him to assess every woman who came his way, particularly if they came his way in the line of business. He supposed if Tallia Venables could read his thoughts, she'd be justified in calling him sexist. She was here as an inventor looking for money. He had no evidence that she was looking for a husband.

"How did you lose your university funding?" he asked, taking the conversation from the general down to business.

Tallia shrugged. "Sexual harassment, really," she said, without thinking. "I said no to my research supervisor once too often, and he got back at me that way."

Brad sat there a minute and then dropped his eyes to his plate. "If you've got a case, why don't you take it to the Commission?"

Tallia said, "Because I already have a career." She

almost said, *two careers.* "I don't need another one arguing my case in front of the Human Rights Commission, which seems to take years. Anyway, I'm quite happy not to be working with Henry anymore. I was always nervous about telling him what I was working on in case he tried to steal it, and that's no good in research. It's inhibiting."

Brad nodded. This explanation made him comfortable. There was no accounting for tastes, and he guessed some men liked to force women, whatever their physical charms, just as a power thing. But somehow to hear her talk so calmly about sexual harassment, looking the way she did...well, he believed her, but it seemed weird.

He wondered briefly if she dressed the way she did because of the sexual harassment, and that, too, seemed to explain the anomaly in a way he could accept.

"What kind of thing are you working on?" he asked.

She paused. "I've got several possible projects, but the one I think you'd be most interested in is in the area of Virtual Reality. It's also the one that's closest to completion." She put down her fork and reached for the briefcase on the floor by her feet. "I've had a lawyer draw this up."

He took the paper and read a more-or-less conventionally worded document stating that he, Brad Slinger, had first heard the ideas in the attached document from...blah blah blah. He reached into his inside pocket, pulled out a pen, and signalled the maitre d'. When the attentive host appeared at his right hand, he said, "Would you mind witnessing a signature, François?"

He made space on the table beside his plate and signed, and then the maitre d' signed and wrote his name and address and Brad handed the document back to Tallia. The maitre d', looking at Tallia curiously, disappeared.

"Right," Brad said.

Tallia rested her elbows on the table and put her chin on her folded hands. "Virtual Reality holidays," she announced softly. "This is something you could install in your Fitness Now clubs, when we get it up and running. We give stressed-out people an hour in a tropical paradise, without leaving Vancouver."

Brad sat forward. "And how do we do that?"

"How familiar are you with Virtual Reality techniques?" she asked.

"I've had a helmet on a few times to shoot up some invaders. My cousin's kids are into it at the moment."

"Right. Well, for Virtual Reality holidays, basically we put a helmet on you that gives you a tropical beach scene. And you're in a room with a wave pool that's got sand underfoot, and full spectrum lighting—that means something that reproduces full sunlight as closely as possible."

"Isn't that dangerous?" asked Brad.

"Lack of full spectrum lighting is what gives people SAD," she said. "This light won't be as strong as the tropical sun, but with the addition of heat lamps, it'll feel like it. We won't bump up the UV, so they won't get a tan."

"Sounds like you've got most of it ironed out already. What's still to do?"

"There are quite a few logistical problems. One, I have to get the full spectrum lighting into the eyes, because the evidence suggests it's the eyes that suffer most from lack of sunlight, although there's no doubt the body needs it, too. So I've got to get that past the Virtual Reality setup, and that's a bit tricky. Two, I have to find a way to match up the scene in the VR hood with the actual wave pool and sand. Do you see what I mean?''

Brad drank, nodding. ''So that when a wave washes them in the wave pool what they see in the hood is a wave.''

She was glad to find him so quick. ''That's right. That's probably the single biggest wrinkle still to go.'' After a little more discussion, she fell silent, letting him think. After a moment, Brad nodded.

''How long till completion, and what do you need?'' he asked then. It was a kooky idea, but he kind of liked it. She was right, it was something that would probably go down well in his gyms. Wave pools would be the biggest expense after the research, and he'd need to cost it all out. But even if he didn't go for this one, the few minutes of discussion had told him Tallia might be worth setting up in a lab of some kind and just giving her a free hand.

They discussed the kind of lab setup she needed, possible costs, and how long she thought she needed to produce a working model. By that time they were at the coffee stage, and Brad was going to be late for a meeting at his office. He signalled for the bill.

''Right. Has my assistant got your phone number?'' he asked.

Tallia flinched. ''I don't think so.''

''Phone her and give it to her. I've got to get back to the office,'' he said, carelessly adding the tip and signing the bill. ''I like this. I'll call you in a day or two. You said something about other projects.''

Tallia said hastily, ''If you decide against this, I've something completely different, but more long term. Non-fossil fuel dependent transportation, for one. And several in between.''

He nodded. "Right. Sorry I don't have more time now. I'll get back to you in a couple of days." He stood up, touched his forefinger to his forehead, said to the hovering maitre d', "François, see that the—ah, the inventor of the future here finds a cab, will you? Put it on my tab."

Before the other man had time to do more than say, "Of course, Mr.—" Brad grinned, nodded, and was gone.

"Will you have more coffee, madame?" François asked, with respect in his voice that hadn't been there an hour and a half ago.

"Thank you," she smiled. "I will."

She sat at the table for another ten minutes, savouring the moment and the hopes that Brad Slinger's attitude had raised in her. Why on earth hadn't she thought of this before? He had treated her throughout the meeting like a scientist, not like a woman at all. He'd respected her brain. He'd been able to focus on ideas without sex getting in the way. There had been no hint of sexual attraction between them. He'd been miles from saying "kiss me" in that abrupt, intense way that had nearly made her heart fibrillate.

Unconsciously, she sighed. It just went to prove that his reaction to Natasha Fox had been entirely based on the physical, Tallia thought. He probably didn't know whether she even had character or personality, let alone finding it attractive. And she was sure *Natasha's* brains had been completely lost on him, though he'd been quick to admire Tallia's.

She wasn't sure why this train of thought should depress her. After all, it only went to prove what she'd always believed.

4

"Come out with me."

The command was delivered in a low, quiet voice, but there was no disguising the urgency behind it. Tallia felt shivers along her arms, and the phone seemed to burn her hand.

"No," she said coldly. "How did you—" she suddenly remembered her role "—you all get this number, anyway?"

"You know how I got it. Your friend told me he was going to tell you."

"He had no business giving it to you, and you had no right to ask for it, Mistah Slinger."

"The hell I didn't," was all he said to that. "Dinner, that's all I'm asking. Are you free tonight?"

"I am not free anytime to you."

"Why not?"

Well, unless she was going to confess everything, that was unanswerable. Tallia hated the fact that she had no quick response, because now he was laughing in her ear, very softly, as if he had won a point.

"Because Ah don't like you," she said, too late for truth.

"You do," said Brad Slinger.

"Nice to think your money gives you influence everywhere,'' she commented dryly, and immediately regretted the words, because if he ever did connect Natasha Fox, actress, with Tallia Venables, inventor, that might count against her. But his arrogant assumption that he attracted her annoyed her. It was a kind of classic response of men, in her experience. If she had a dollar for every man who'd said "Baby, you're dying for it," or some equivalent, she wouldn't need Brad Slinger's money.

The fact that, for once, it was only the truth didn't alter her anger. Increased it, maybe.

"I don't think my money gives me influence everywhere," he returned, and now there was bite in his tone. This, she thought, a little nervously, was the man who made boardrooms quail. "Is that a hint?"

She gasped at the implication. "What? No!"

"I'll consider putting in a bid," he said.

"No bid from you all is going to change mah mind, Mr. Slinger," she said, somewhat rashly.

"Oh, I think it might," he contradicted her.

The rudeness was deliberate. Tallia could feel the steam coming out her ears. "How dare you!"

"You're an actress, after all."

She hung up, furious, but almost glad he had made it so easy for her. It would be the height of stupidity for Natasha Fox to think she could date Brad Slinger without getting into seriously hot water, and anyway, Tallia reminded herself, she didn't want to. A man whose reaction to her was entirely based on the physical was just what she did not need.

And the complications were just plain unthinkable.

Brad slowly cradled the phone and sat mentally kicking himself. What the hell kind of approach was that to a woman? Not a winning one, for sure, but somehow

Natasha Fox got under his skin. After a lifetime of never dating actresses, he'd broken his rule only to find that the actress in question wouldn't date him! It was infuriating.

It wasn't that he hadn't had his share of rejections, though it was true that these got fewer as his bank balance rose. Brad told himself that was it—he wasn't used to rejection, so Natasha Fox's had caught him on his soft underbelly. Well, there was an easy answer to that. He would just forget her. He'd been a fool to break the rule of a lifetime, anyway. There were lots more beautiful women in the world than Natasha Fox seemed to imagine. More than there were rich men, he was pretty sure. So to hell with her. It wasn't as if he was death-defyingly attracted to her or anything like that. He couldn't imagine why he'd said all that about putting in a bid. Sheer temper, he supposed. It would be a cold day in hell before he made a money offer for any woman.

Five minutes later he caught himself wishing he'd asked her what brand of perfume she'd been using that night in the car. Boy, that was some stuff! He'd about lost his head completely. He'd sure like to get hold of some of whatever it was.

"Oh, wow! This is fantastic!"

Tallia turned her glowing face towards Brad and remembered just in time to smile with her mouth closed over her fake teeth. "This is wonderful!"

Call it The Dream Lab. Twice the floor space she'd told him she would need, at least, Tallia could see that at a glance. And full of light and air, with high ceilings and broad windows as well as the last word in indirect lighting. Computers whose descriptions she'd only sighed over at the university. Drawing boards and work stations…and her very own private office with a desk and everything else that might inhabit a budding inventor's dreams.

"I'm glad you like it," he said.

"But—it's so big! It's so much more than I expected. I mean—the cost—"

"I wish everybody would stop talking about money!" Brad exploded irritably. "Sorry," he said immediately, as Tallia blinked. "I've got something on my mind." A woman, that was what he had on his mind. It was two weeks since his conversation with Natasha Fox and he still hadn't got her out of his head. "Don't worry about your budget, the rent for this won't come out of it. I own the building, and I can write it off."

"Well, it's just wonderful!" Tallia said again. "You just don't know what this means to me." She stroked the smooth surface of a tilted drawing board, pushing a little plastic marker along the length of a ruler, and he thought that it was as if she were stroking a lover.

Suddenly he remembered that ridiculous conversation he'd had with Jake, about wanting to fall for a woman with brains. He'd said then that he would like to fall in love with Tallia, though he hadn't met her yet. And then he'd stupidly let Jake talk him into going to that premiere…. That had been his big mistake. If he'd never met Natasha Fox, if instead he'd stuck to that wild idea—he might have found himself attracted to Tallia.

Well, it wasn't too late.

"Will you have dinner with me?" he said abruptly.

Tallia, who was tapping into a computer by this time, turned a startled face to him. Brad kicked himself for his approach. He hoped he wasn't going to lose all his finesse with women just because one blond bombshell had turned him down.

"Pardon?" she asked, a little breathlessly.

"Are you free for dinner tonight?"

She stood straight and looked at him, brown eyes against muddy hair, badly made up and a not-very-good figure. He'd never dated anyone so physically unaware in his life. He supposed it was the scientific mind—the female counterpart of the absentminded professor.

"On what basis, Brad?" she asked gently. "Is this business?"

"No, it is not business! It's pleasure, or I would like to think so!" he returned, more irritably than the situation called for. "Will you have dinner with me, that's the question?"

Tallia's heart was beating hard, and her brain just wouldn't kick into action at all. She stared at him blankly, her mouth half open. Was it possible? Was she hearing right? Brad Slinger wanted to date her? Dressed and made up the way she was?

Tallia never forgot that she was in her plain disguise, because the reaction—or rather the lack of reaction— from men around her was a constant reminder. They simply ignored her. She was invisible. Sometimes this was a tremendous relief, and she couldn't understand why she had never thought of disguise before. But sometimes it angered her, too. She wanted to shake them, and say, *I am exactly the same woman underneath!*

And now, here was Brad Slinger—Tallia felt a smile pull the corners of her mouth.

She caught herself abruptly. She couldn't date him. How could she? No matter how careful she was, in close, intimate situations her disguise was bound to slip. Suppose he was really attracted? She was pretty sure her false teeth would be detectable in a kiss.

The thought of Brad kissing her burned her cheeks.

She dropped her eyes. "I'm sorry, Brad," she said softly. Her heart beat even harder in protest. Was there ever going to be any way out of this?

Brad remembered suddenly that she had told him she'd suffered sexual harassment at the university. There had been a look in her eyes just now, haunted almost—though just for a moment he'd thought she was going to say yes in spite of it—that made him wonder what form the harassment had taken.

"Why not?" he asked gently.

"I just don't—" She realized she was about to come out with the trite "don't think it would be a good idea" and saw what kind of argument that might lead to. Her resistance was feeble and he was experienced enough to suss that out pretty quickly. She said instead, "don't date" in what she hoped was a very firm voice.

It was suddenly all crystal clear to Brad, the reason for the unattractive clothes and the failure to make anything of her good points. She was a woman on the run, from her own sexuality and everyone else's, and it was some man's fault. He was pretty sure it wouldn't do any good to pressure her, not now anyway.

"I'm sorry to hear that," he said, and began talking about hiring an assistant for her.

He took Tallia's rejection a lot easier than Natasha's, Tallia told herself cynically. Her heart sank at the thought that she had turned down her one chance to date a man who was—however weakly—actually attracted to her brain.

Jake reached lazily across the table, picked up another oyster, cracked and ate it. "Man, it's a real education to watch you handle women," he observed. "So, you jumped her in the back of the limousine, and now she won't speak to you." He shook his head, grinning. "Where were you when they gave out the rules?"

Brad frowned irritably. "Dammit, I know the rules! I don't know what happened. It must have been the perfume she was wearing."

Jake snapped another oyster. "It was that 40 triple D cup, my friend, why don't you admit it? And the big blue eyes and the hair and the legs…you lost it, boy, so what are you going to do about it?"

"I'll get over it," Brad insisted.

"Not without bedding her, you won't. I could maybe help there," he added, with a certain interest.

"You stay out of it," Brad ordered.

"Ha! You see? Jealous! Brad, you know what?" Jake sat back and eyed his friend with misgiving. "I think you've really lost it. I think your carefree bachelor days are over. This is when you start writing bad poetry."

"I am not in love with an actress and I am not going to fall in love with an actress," Brad said mulishly.

"There's a kind of psychological resonance in it that I like," Jake went on, as if he hadn't spoken.

"And I am certainly not going to write poetry about it," Brad said, demolishing his fine stand.

"I've always said you were mother-ridden, and this just—"

"I am much more likely to fall in love with Tallia."

"You told me she's ugly," Jake reminded him ruthlessly.

"I did not tell you she's ugly. She's got looks, but her confidence needs boosting."

"More than her confidence, the way I read it. Maybe she could borrow some of what Natasha Fox puts in her bra. She's got enough for two." Jake warmed to his subject.

"You haven't even met her, Jake."

"I don't have to meet her to know that if you put them side by side, Brad, you'd go for Natasha Fox every time. If you were being honest with yourself."

"That's all surface. Once I got to know them, I think I might make a different choice."

Jake sat up, dropped his oyster knife, and shot him with both hands. "Right! Let's put your money where your mouth is! How would you like to place a little bet on that?"

"Nash, darling, it's me."

"Damon! Ili!" Tallia exclaimed. "How's the fund-raising?"

There was a pause, and she was immediately sorry she'd asked the question. "Not good, eh?"

"Well, Nash, it could be very good. But that kind of depends on you."

"On me! What now?" She laughed, but a little thrill of premonitory fear chased along the skin of her shoulders and breasts.

"I've just had a meeting with your friend Brad Slinger."

The name acted on her just like an electric shock. She felt the vibration travel from the receiver up her arm and to her left ear and breast. Her reaction frightened her. So did the knowledge that Brad Slinger was not giving up. She had hung up on him three times running, and it got harder every time.

"I don't want to hear this, Damon," Tallia warned.

"You don't know what he's offering."

"I don't *care* what he's offering, Damon! I am not going to be bribed by a man who's only after one thing, as my grandmother used to say."

"He told me he'll be satisfied with just your company," the director pleaded.

She thought of him saying, *kiss me,* and shivered. "He lied to you. It's glorified prostitution he's offering, so you know what that makes you, Damon?"

"Darling, darling Nash, please will you listen to what he offered? Just listen?"

Tallia heaved a fulminating sigh. "The answer is going to be no, Damon, but you go ahead and tell me if you want."

"He'll back me to the tune of fifty thousand dollars for every time you see him, if you see him for five dates," Damon said flatly.

Tallia gasped. *"What?"* She choked on saliva and coughed. "What?" she demanded somewhat more mildly when she could speak again. "Is he completely out of his mind, or are you?" She paused. "Or am I?"

"Natasha, that's a quarter of a million dollars. With a vote of confidence like that from Brad Slinger, I'll have backers lined up to bankroll me. I could make The Film this year. Please."

She didn't ask what film, because everyone who knew Damon knew that he had a dream film he was dying to make when he got enough money. A film he couldn't make for under a million.

What she desperately wanted to know was what all this would mean for the future of her lab. Just how much money did Brad Slinger have to throw around? The thought that it was her own refusal to date him that had caused him to offer Damon financing was almost too bitter to bear. If she said yes now, would the quarter million be taken out of her lab? And if she went on saying no, would he up the bid, and *then* take it out of her lab?

This was enough to drive anyone absolutely crazy. If she'd known it would come to this, she'd have said yes to a date before, whatever the risk.

"Damon, please don't ask me to see this man. You don't know what he's like," she begged.

The director said nothing, and she was silent herself, remembering how much she owed him. As a nearly complete country innocent, arriving into the theatrical community in Vancouver at the age of seventeen, she had been very, very lucky to run into Damon Picton...but he would not remind her of that, she knew.

When the silence grew to unbearable proportions, she said, "I'll think about it, Damon," and put the phone down on his premature expressions of gratitude.

"Oh, boy!" said Bel theatrically. "What are you going to do?"

"I don't know," Tallia groaned. "How did I ever get into this? I don't understand how I got into this."

"Oh what a tangled web you wove."

"Bel, I need help, not Shakespearean paraphrases."

"Sir Walter Scott," Bel corrected her tolerantly. "It's from *Marmion*."

"I don't need him, either."

"Tal, you can't start dating Brad Slinger, so just say no."

"You don't know how much I owe Damon."

"No, that's true. How much do you owe Damon?" Bel demanded brightly.

Tal sat silent, remembering those long-ago days. "Men were just all over me, from the moment I went to my first audition," she said.

She had been lucky to meet Damon almost at once. He understood what was happening, and almost before she knew it, she and Damon were pretending to be engaged. This had considerably reduced the number of offers, since few men had the brass to try and get past her sweet-eyed "I don't think my fiancé would like that." It had stopped entirely the near assaults. Damon Picton was an unknown quantity, volatile and with a long memory.

He had saved her from what she knew now would have been a very unpleasant period in her life. She really had been too innocent to understand, and too polite to be able to protect herself effectively.

He had asked nothing of her in return. After a few months, when Tallia had found her sea legs, the engagement had been quietly forgotten.

"So what was in it for him?" Bel demanded when she could listen no longer. "Is he gay?"

"No, I'm pretty sure it isn't that," Tallia said, reflecting that Bel was a good deal less innocent than she had been at a similar age. "I kind of wondered at the time whether—" She paused, thinking, and at Bel's prodding, went on. "I did think that maybe he'd had his heart broken or something, and that was his way of hiding. But I really had no reason to think it. It was just something about him."

"So now you feel you owe him."

"Damon would never say so. And that's not the worst problem, either. I mean, if I do it, where's the money going to come from? Will he take it from my lab?"

"You're right. Even Brad Slinger can't be that rich." Bel's hands flew to her cheeks in overdone horror. "Boy, are you stuck!"

Tallia said dryly, "Stop enjoying it so much!"

"Sorry, sis, but honestly, how do you get into these things?"

Tallia narrowed her eyes at her younger sister. "Partly through listening to my kid sister, whose idea this was in the first place!"

"Apart from that," Bel riposted.

"What's your favourite dinner?" Brad Slinger asked, carefully keeping triumph out of his tone.

"Anything eaten in a very public place," Natasha Fox said coldly. "Let me make it plain that this deal does not include intimate little dinners or private entertainments, Mr. Slinger."

"You seem to have a very low opinion of the male sex, or is it just me?"

"Y'all do realize that this is blackmail," she said.

There was a startled silence at the other end of the phone. "Blackmail? Who's blackmailing you? Damon Picton?" Brad demanded fiercely. The ferocity was mostly directed at himself for not realizing that this was a possibility.

"You all are, for goodness sakes!" Tallia exploded, finding it hard to express anger through the Honey Childe accent. She wondered if that was why Southern women always seemed so pleasant.

"I am not blackmailing anyone," Brad said flatly, astonished to discover how quickly this woman could make him furious. Or anything else. He was like a teenager, completely unable to control his emotions. "Who says I am?"

"Ah say you are! Fifty thousand every time Ah date you! What do y'all call that if not blackmail?"

"I call that bribery," Brad said dangerously.

"You'll pardon me if Ah don't see the difference."

"There is quite a difference, nevertheless, which you

may appreciate if you ever happen to become the victim of a blackmailer. Let's hope you never do.''

''Probably Ah'm laying myself open to it right now, being paid to date you all!'' Tallia said hotly. ''Ah surely will want to keep that out of the public eye, let me tell you.''

''If anyone tries to blackmail you with regard to this, you send them to me,'' Brad Slinger said.

A snort was all that greeted that, and she had a point. If this story got out, Brad reflected, he would look like a very big fool, and what would Natasha Fox look like? Worse than a fool, for sure.

''All right,'' he said. ''If you'll give me your word to see me for five dates, no more, I'll tell your director it was just a joke and bankroll him now,'' Brad said, wondering where his hormones would lead him next. Maybe this was premature senility or something? He ought to find himself a nice woman and settle down before the effects became more noticeable. Maybe he would marry his inventor. If she'd have him.

''Ah'll give you my word if you all give me yours,'' Natasha Fox said.

''On what?''

''That sex is not part of this deal. That you all don't, at any time, try to kiss me or…or make love to me or consider that you've purchased anything except extremely platonic company over five dinners.''

Brad stared into the middle distance, then blew out a breath. ''Let's say, I won't do anything without your permission.''

She laughed in genuine amusement. ''Oh, now, Mr. Slinger, men always do imagine they have a woman's permission. 'Your mouth says no, but your eyes are saying yes,' you all ever used that on a girl?''

Only in the dim distant past, but Brad cringed nonetheless.

"All right, dammit, if you ask me, then."

"If Ah ask you straight out, and in words of one syllable," she amended gently.

"All right. Deal," he said irritably, because this was certainly going to put a crimp in his plans for getting Natasha Fox out of his system. It wasn't the bet that Jake had insisted on making that made him so determined to see Natasha. It was the knowledge that she was a woman who might haunt a man for the rest of his life. He refused to be one of those men who'd seen their dream woman but not done anything about it, and regretted it for the rest of their days. He had always believed that such men thrived on the dream, and if they'd ever actually met the woman the dream would have died under the weight of reality. And he was going to kill his dream.

"What is it you want?" Tallia demanded after a moment. She wasn't happy with this. She had been hoping to take a stand that would allow her to refuse, and tell Damon why. "What are you expecting five dates to prove?"

"That's my business."

She observed, with more heat than, on the surface, the event demanded, "I suppose all your other charities are going to suffer for this? Your investments and your orphans or whatever it is?" It was said that Brad Slinger was pretty generous to charity, though his donations were never made public.

"This money is free money, not earmarked for anything else, so you can rest easy," he said. "My orphans, as you call them, are safe. Now, where shall I pick you up?"

5

"This is kinda risky, isn't it?" Bel said.

Tallia concentrated on fixing a false eyelash in place, then glanced at her sister in the mirror. "Yes, it's kinda risky," she agreed ironically. "What do you suggest I do?"

She didn't mean that literally, but Bel nibbled at her lower lip. "Why don't you play really dumb? Maybe he'll get bored before the five dates are up—and before he susses out your disguise."

"That's what I like—the old Venables vote of confidence."

"It stands to reason, Tal. The more you see him, the worse your chances are. It's got nothing to do with how good an actress you are."

"You're talking about my life here."

"Why don't you confess, then? Just stop now and tell him all about it. He might just laugh."

"Yeah, all the way to the bank, where he's telling them my line of credit is no good anymore."

"Yeah, but—"

"Men hate being made fools of, am I right?" Tallia said inarguably, swinging around on the dressing stool. "How do I look?"

"Very enhanced."

"Let's hope he doesn't try and pull any of it off. It might come." Tallia grinned. The grin was just a cover for her terrible nerves, and she was relieved when it fooled Bel.

Bel was right about that "enhanced." Natasha was almost a caricature of glamour tonight. Blue contact lenses that matched her silk dress made her eyes a bright, impossible blue, and had the added benefit of somehow hiding the soul behind. Her silk dress clung to curves, but the matching jacket disguised such telltale features as her shoulders and the line of her back. Her big-hair wig was squeezed and gelled in a froth of curls that fell all around her face, neck and shoulders, hiding the shape of her jaw and ears. The enhanced bra pushed up her breasts and added several cup sizes, and her slip-on stilettos made her inches taller.

The most difficult area was hands. There was nothing she could do to disguise them except add brightly painted stick-on talons, two heavy bracelets, and as many rings as would fit.

"This is my sister, Bel," she said a few minutes later, introducing Brad Slinger. "We room together," she added, in case he had any ideas about bringing her home tonight. The two girls had decided that Natasha Fox would use Bel's apartment as her home address. It meant hiding all Bel's university notebooks and anything else that had the name Annabel Venables scrawled on it.

Bel grinned up at Brad, obviously liking what she saw. "Hi there," she said. "I guess you know if you harm a hair of her head you've got me to deal with."

"I do now." He smiled and then narrowed his eyes. "You remind me of someone."

Bel pouted and pushed her hair up and tried to look

as unlike Tallia and as like Natasha as possible. "My sister, maybe," she suggested hopefully.

He shook his head. "Yes, but that's not it. Someone else."

"You're not very flattering." Bel dropped her hands. "Sorry, can't help. We've got a big family back home, but they don't come to the city much."

Natasha was suddenly eager to leave the apartment, a fact Brad noticed and thought he guessed the reason for. He smiled at Bel and followed Natasha's entrancingly swaying hips out into the corridor.

He was absolutely determined to control himself with her from now on, and so he walked beside her to the elevator and didn't touch her once. He knew damned well he could get this out of his system, given time.

He tried not to stare down into her cleavage as he ushered her into the low red Porsche. For a woman who wasn't interested in him, she sure did dress to attract, he reflected. Her slim blue dress was the thinnest silk he'd ever seen, and although it wasn't tight, it clung to her body at all the right places. Underneath the light matching jacket he saw spaghetti straps, and wondered if the restaurant would be warm enough to make her take it off.

But when he slipped into the driver's seat and moved a hand to put the car in gear, he noticed that her knees were slanted away, well out of casual reach.

"How's your meal?"

"Oh, just fine, thank you," Natasha replied distantly, scarcely flicking him with that blue gaze. She seemed completely self-absorbed, only speaking when asked a direct question. She kept her head tilted down, even when she spoke to him, so that mostly what he saw was hair. His logical brain, always slow to function in her presence, stirred with a distant, belated curiosity: just why was she so reluctant to date him? Brad reminded himself that the deal had been for dinner and no more, but still, he was annoyed. She'd seemed a fairly interesting person the first time he'd met her. But he'd tried her on several topics and she had simply smiled vapidly and said, "That's very interesting," or "Ah really wouldn't know about that," and offered nothing.

Of course, he shouldn't be annoyed about it. He should be grateful. Natasha Fox was the last person he wanted to be seriously attracted to, and at this rate the spell she seemed to have cast on him might be broken after one date.

Only instead he found the hunter in him being intrigued. He was sure she was in there, hiding from him. He wanted her to come out.

Tallia had taken Bel's suggestion about playing dumb, and there were two ways to do that—by talking too much about nothing, or by not talking. The former would have come easier to her, but she figured the less she talked, the less danger there was of him recognizing her voice. It had scared her rigid when Brad had told Bel she reminded him of someone, because that someone could only be Tallia Venables.

It wasn't easy answering in monosyllables, though, especially as Brad seemed to be more intelligent than the average rich man, and a thinker about things. As well as being so strong-looking and kind of rugged handsome, with eyes that just burned her up over the table. She actually had to defocus her eyes as she listened, in order to minimize his purely physical impact on her. She smiled a lot, as vapidly as possible, and being careful to show her teeth. The closed-mouth smile was Tallia's.

"How many brothers and sisters do you have?" Brad asked suddenly.

She threw him a startled look, and the inward-turning Siamese-cat gaze was replaced by alertness. "Five," she said. "Well, that is, we're five altogether."

"Your sister doesn't have as much of an accent as you," he observed.

"No, the younger ones were raised here. But Ah was older when Ah came, and Ah go back home a lot."

They were all lies, but what else could she do? And it was a reasonable explanation for why her own accent kept slipping. Tallia knew it was crucial to keep him off the subject of her. "What about you? Are y'all part of a big family?"

"No, I was an only child. My mother left when I was three and my father didn't remarry until just recently. His wife has children, but I don't know them very well."

"Your mother left you? Oh, that's tragic! Why?"

Brad's eyes dropped to his plate. "To seek her fortune in Hollywood."

"Oh." Natasha was silent again, taking that in. After a moment she looked right into his eyes, her head a little on one side. "What are y'all doing with me, then?"

"I like you."

When he said it like that, just a bald fact, gazing right into her eyes, she could feel it all the way to her toes. Tallia shivered and tried to keep her grip. He was looking particularly masculine this evening, too, his black hair falling down over one eye, his strong jaw freshly shaved, and smelling of Eau Sauvage. She grasped firmly at reality. "Do y'all hate your mother for what she did?"

For a long time, he had. A long, long, unprofitable time. Brad shrugged. "Why should I hate her? She was doing what she wanted to do, and that's supposed to be the right thing, isn't it?''

"Not where Ah come from," Tallia said firmly. She meant the little town nestled in the mountains behind Whistler, but of course he took her to mean Tennessee or Alabama.

"She was married at nineteen and had a baby at twenty, before she had any idea about life, she told me once. And it didn't suit her. She was very pretty, and a talent scout convinced her to try her luck in Hollywood.''

"And how was her luck?" Natasha demanded dryly. "Do Ah know her name?''

"You don't, but her luck was pretty good. She lives in complete luxury, and looks about ten years older than you. She couldn't give up her career for family, but she did it fast enough for money. She married again, a wealthy producer twice her age, who is still turning out winners at the age of seventy-five or so." He told her the famous name, watching for the inevitable reaction. He wondered how long it would take her to ask for an introduction. Surreptitiously he glanced at his watch.

"Do they have children?''

"No. Once was enough for my mother. He's got a few from his previous marriages.''

"Ah guess y'all don't see much of them.''

Here it comes, Brad thought. *The pitch.* He glanced at his watch again. Thirty-two seconds.

"Not much." Some of them he'd never met.

"Y'all should meet my mother," Natasha said. "She said she made the choice to have a family so she figured she might as well do it all out. That's why she had five of us. Y'all'd like her.''

Full marks for novelty of approach, Brad told himself.

Fifty-one seconds. "Thank you. I'd like to," he said instantly.

Suddenly Tallia heard what she had just said. What on earth was she thinking of? Was she crazy, letting her guard down like that, chatting away about her family? Inviting him to meet her mother, of all things! It was because his story had stirred her pity.

"Oh, well, Ah don't suppose…" she stammered, trying to recover lost ground.

No, I didn't think you did, Brad told her with silent amusement. One minute thirteen. He decided to put her out of her misery.

"Maybe you'd like to meet my stepfather one day. I'm sure he'd like to meet you."

She frowned with surprise. "Your *step*father?"

"Yes. Wouldn't you like to meet him?"

Tallia shrugged, wondering what on earth he could mean. "Well, it just seems odd that y'all say your stepfather, and not your own father."

"My father is not a famous Hollywood producer."

So far was she from any real interest in a film career, Tallia only looked at him blankly. "Ah'm not much of a celebrity hunter," she said apologetically.

Brad's eyebrows came together as he gazed at her. "But you are an actress."

Tallia blushed bright red, she could feel it. Her hands flew to her cheeks. "Oh! Oh! Yes, Ah see! Ah'm afraid Ah just never thought of that!"

He couldn't believe his ears. Was she as devious as this seemed to suggest, or was she really so blind to her chances?

"Well, think of it now," he invited her softly. Maybe shipping her off to Hollywood would be the smart thing to do. Out of sight, out of mind. And at least he'd know where he stood. He wouldn't be always waiting for the axe to fall.

Brad saw where his thoughts had led him and drew himself up short. He would not be waiting for any axe to fall, because he was not going to get seriously involved with Natasha Fox. He was going to bed her and get her out of his system after a few dates.

Tallia smiled and feigned interest. "Thank you, that really is a very kind thought. Someday, maybe," she said.

Brad frowned curiously at her. There was something very mysterious about Natasha Fox. His interest in her, which he had hoped to kill, was increasing by the hour.

He played the radio in the car on the way home, a golden oldies station that played romantic, sexy music late at night. There had been nothing in the rules against music. Night fell late in Vancouver in July, so he had made sure to linger over the meal till there would be darkness, the smooth velvety darkness of a perfect summer night. He rolled down the windows and took the long way, driving slowly along the sea. Then, though it wasn't in his plans, he pulled up and stopped, not in any secluded place that could make her object, but on the boulevard that bordered the sea wall. He killed the engine. The music was still playing, softly and insistently, but now the sounds of the sea blended with it.

"Can I be sure? I need to know," sang a voice with haunting sexuality. Tallia sighed in spite of herself, her guard well down. Brad had not underestimated the effect of the best food and wine, the perfume of the night, and moody melody. Nor the fact that he had not tried to touch her or otherwise breach their contract all night.

"This is my parents' favourite song," Tallia said, suddenly suffused with a yearning for home and family. It was time for another visit to that warm comfort that had bred her and nurtured her. But her yearning went deeper than that tonight. The song made her want love in her own life, the kind that had kept her parents together through good times and bad, able to laugh even in the worst moments, because love was the root of their connection to each other and the universe.

Brad let her sit in silence till the song was over. "Care for a stroll?" he said then. She glanced over at him in the shadows, and he lifted both hands in silent promise. She smiled at him from the depths of a nostalgia for what hadn't yet happened to her, and Brad began to wonder if he could be certain that she would crack before he did.

"All right," she whispered.

It would be impossible to walk long in Natasha's stilettos, but fortunately she wasn't wearing stockings. In the darkness she slipped her feet out of her shoes as Brad walked around the car to open the door for her.

The day had been hot, and the pavement was warm underfoot. Brad took off his jacket and tossed it into the car before locking it.

There were many people on the sea wall, couples of all sorts and descriptions, but in the darkness they were alone together. Brad didn't speak, content just to be with her, her perfume reaching his nostrils along with the sea smell and the sometime scent of flowers.

The tide was high, splashing only a few feet below the top of the wall, sending up spray where there were rocks in its way, and sometimes touching them with a fine mist, cool on their heated skin. Now and then they had to dodge the splash of a bigger wave.

A couple were on the grass on the other side of the path, rolling together in a passionate, drunken kiss it was impossible not to be aware of. There was a sound of lips parting, and then a girl whimpered a boy's name on a note of sexual excitement that electrified the air.

There were two who seemed to have found the one they were looking for, Tallia thought, as her nameless yearning deepened. For Brad, meanwhile, the soft female cry had operated on his system as if it had come from Natasha's mouth, and his loins leapt painfully.

He grimaced and tried to steer his mind away from the shoals of thinking if he just pulled her down on the grass she couldn't resist him.

Someone walked by with a radio playing very softly. "The smell of her deep black hair," chanted a man with passionate intensity. "Full of my whispered words."

Suddenly it seemed as if the whole world were conspiring against their celibacy, against the distance between them, as if it were some violation of the night. Tallia was suddenly very aware of the bulk of muscle that the short sleeves and thin fabric of Brad's shirt revealed.

"Are you barefoot?" he asked, suddenly noticing. His voice was tight with strain, the sexual strain of wanting to touch her. The knowledge that she had taken off her shoes, the thought of her long, naked legs, almost hurt.

It seemed that the expression of his desire would always trigger hers, and Tallia suddenly, almost unbearably, wanted him to kiss her.

She swallowed and coughed to clear the frog in her throat. "Yes, I—Ah can't walk far in those things." She nodded to underline her speech, a little habit she had that he had noticed, and the moonlight, freeing itself from cloud suddenly, got caught in the tangles of her hair. He leaned closer and inhaled its scent. It nearly killed him.

"I want to kiss you," he told her hoarsely.

Something gold pulsed and glittered against her breast in the moonlight, and he knew that she was trembling. "Brad, y'all gave me your word," she whispered.

"Yes, I did," he said. "Release me from it. I want to kiss you. Christ, kiss you? I want to—" He choked off the words. "Lie down with me," he urged. "The grass is warm."

She was saved by the thought of her wig. She was pretty sure it would stay on if she lay down, but if Brad started pulling it, it would come off in his hand. "You promised," Tallia managed to stammer.

His desire moved towards anger. "Why not?" he demanded fiercely. "Why can't I kiss you?"

"Ah told you why."

"Tell me again."

"Because Ah don't want you to."

"Liar," he said brutally.

She gasped. "Ah think you'd better take me home."

He stopped, took her arm, turned her to face him. "Ask me to kiss you," he growled. "Say it. *Brad, kiss me.* Say it."

As she twisted to pull her arm out of his grasp, a giant wave smashed itself against the rocks below them, splayed up, and drenched Tallia. She reeled and staggered, and he naturally caught her. Just as naturally, once his arms were around her, he dragged her against him.

Then they stood frozen for a moment, wet and shocked, their senses electrified, staring into the moonlight of each other's eyes. She felt his body pulsing with excitement against hers, he felt her shiver with deep physical awareness.

Perhaps it was the cold water, but, even aroused as he

was, he now had control. He grinned, his face wet, his teeth glistening.

"You're beautiful when you're soaked," he said. He knew it was inevitable between them. Holding her in his arms, he knew that. He could wait. Like a tiger whose prey is tethered to a stake, he could circle her at his leisure. Only a greedy fool grabbed for what was already his own. She would ask him for everything before he was through.

But his hands on her bare shoulders took in the sensation of slippery skin and wanted more now. "Tell me to kiss you," he urged again.

Tallia was terrified. Inside, somewhere, perhaps she had made the same discovery as he had, but in her brain it translated into danger. "Brad, please...let me go," she said levelly, but there was a quaver in her voice.

"Take all the time you need," Brad said, releasing her. "You're a woman worth waiting for."

She stood straight, futilely pulling her soaked dress away from her skin. She began to shiver in earnest, though the night was still warm. She didn't know what was wrong with her. After a moment she realized it was the thought of Brad Slinger waiting for her that was making her shake so badly.

6

━━━◆◆━━━

"**Y**ou look terrific," Brad said appreciatively.

Tallia fidgeted, a fact which he attributed to discomfort around men but was in fact awkwardness with finding him at her apartment door. The people in the building were just too free about letting strangers in without a key. She had planned to meet him downstairs.

Well, perhaps it was for the best. At least now it would be firmly fixed in his mind that she and Natasha Fox lived in two different apartments.

"Thank you," she said, marvelling at the ease with which the lie came to his lips. She didn't look terrific. In fact, she was amazed at how awful it was possible to look in cheap, ill-fitting clothes and with the help of bad skin, bad teeth and bad hair.

She had not disguised herself as "Tallia" for a while. At first, fearing that Brad might turn up unannounced at the lab, she had faithfully dressed and made up in her plain guise every day. But slowly, as she discovered that Brad's own office was miles away, and it happened that Brad rarely came to the lab, and never unannounced, she had become less rigorous. Then she had hired an assistant, and after that, except for the false teeth and the brown eyes, she left the disguise off, contenting herself with dressing neatly and plainly and without makeup.

She had washed the brown rinse out of her hair, so for tonight she was wearing a wig in a drab colour, certain that Brad had never looked at her long enough or closely enough to know the difference. Mostly she and Brad talked on the phone.

She preferred that. The Tallia disguise was no longer as liberating as it had once been, or at least not around Brad. In fact, she had found it irksome to feel his eyes slide over her without any real sign of heat or interest. And she certainly preferred not to listen to the kind of lie he had just told her.

Brad forgot who had told him the golden rule of speaking to the intent, and not to the result. It arose effortlessly from his subconscious just when he needed it, though. *No one* wants *to turn in a bad performance,* whoever it was had said. *So when I say they were great, it's not a lie. What I'm really saying is, I can see that they wanted to be great.* And he figured Tallia must have gone to a lot of trouble and wanted to look terrific tonight. So he spoke to the intent.

With a little ripple like electric shock, Brad suddenly realized that it was his mother's advice he was remembering. She had said it once when, visiting her in L.A., he had watched her compliment someone whose performance in a film he knew she had hated. By God, that must be a first, finding wisdom in something his mother had said!

"Is your lawyer downstairs?" Tallia was asking.

"Jake's meeting us there."

The ruse with which he had got her to come out had been a simple one—he'd merely said he needed a business meeting between her and Jake, and booked it for dinner. It might not have worked if Tallia hadn't been completely preoccupied, by a little discovery that might lead anywhere, when he phoned her at the lab.

"It's a question of the angle of refraction in relation to..." she had bubbled excitedly, losing him instantly. But though he didn't understand science, Brad knew women, and he let her run on, explaining and exclaiming.

"Very, very rewarding," he said, when it seemed she had got to the end. "I can see you want to get back to your work. Will you be working all night, or can you make time to meet Jake for dinner?"

Tallia was intent on her computer screen. "Tonight? Yes, all right. Where shall I meet him?"

"Us. I'll be there, too," Brad said smoothly, pleased with how straightforward it sounded. "I'll pick you up. My secretary has your address."

She hadn't even noticed. "Okay, fine."

"Seven?"

He was out of her field of consciousness long before the receiver hit the cradle, Brad knew. The last few weeks weren't doing much for his masculine ego. He was set on two women, and neither of them really cared enough to give him the time of day.

He wasn't sure why he was so set on dating Tallia. Jake was right, he usually liked beautiful women, and yet there was something about Tallia that—intrigued him, maybe. He wasn't sure. The sense that under that exterior there was a person he could get to like, if she stopped guarding herself from him.

She didn't seem to return the compliment. She had turned him down twice, and he had had to resort to subterfuge.

As they entered the elevator now he guided her with a hand on her waist, and then again as he opened the main door, and Tallia reflected that, although *Natasha* had his word on the subject, he had made no deal about not touching *Tallia*. When they walked he was closer to her than he walked with Natasha, too, and she discovered that his nearness was enough to make her skin shiver with awareness. She wished they *had* made some kind of deal, because the last thing she wanted was to get overheated over Brad Slinger.

The sexy red Porsche sat at the curb, and she couldn't help a little noise of appreciation. "Oh, I'm—" she began, and then remembered that Tallia could hardly have fond memories of the Porsche.

"Yes?" he prompted, when she stopped speaking, but she merely sank into the seat and shook her head.

She was interested to discover that he was pulling up at the same restaurant he had taken Natasha to a few nights ago. She knew it was a very "in" place, and she was pretty sure that a lot of men wouldn't be caught dead with someone like her in such a place. Her estimation of him went up, and her heart simultaneously sank. She was already aware of a sexual attraction for Brad. The smart thing would be not to start liking him in addition.

She was smiling at something Brad said, forgetting her closed smile, when they arrived at the table, so Jake got the full benefit of her orthodontically unsound teeth. He'd also tracked their approach, so Jake had more time than Brad had ever taken, he figured, to check out the figure. She was tall but shapeless, her clothes were unbelievable, and her hair was practically in *ringlets*. She looked like the prom photo horrors he'd used to laugh over in his father's high school yearbook.

"Hi," he said, when they had been introduced. "Brad tells me you're going to make his next fortune for him."

He could believe it. There could only be one excuse for a woman being so unaware of fashion and grooming, and that was that she was some kind of genius.

Jake was here tonight as decoy. He was supposed to get an urgent phone call in half an hour and leave, promising to return. Just to make it look good he was to ask Tallia a few ''preliminary questions'' right off the top, and then let the conversation wander, as if there was plenty of time to get down to business. Much later, he'd phone with a message that he couldn't get back.

But Jake had plans of his own. They had been only hazily formulated, but firmed up very quickly when he clapped eyes on Tallia Venables. It wasn't that he didn't think Brad was right, and that she would look at lot better if she tried to make something of herself. But what he knew immediately was that she would never try. A woman who was content to look like this just didn't have *any* natural taste or inclination. If Brad had a *Pygmalion* scenario in the back of his mind he could forget it. You could take this woman to every boutique and beautician in the city, but a week after her transformation she would look like a dog again.

It would not be right, and it certainly wasn't Jake's idea of friendship, to allow his best buddy to fall for the brains or personality of a woman like this. There were plenty of intelligent women around who also had some style sense. Brad would be unhappy—miserable, in fact—in the long run, if he got attached to a woman like this. Hell, he'd be miserable in the *short* run.

And it was up to Jake to protect his friend from the fate he was contemplating. So while Brad was consulting the wine list, Jake opened his briefcase to pull out a yellow legal pad and pen, quietly turned off his phone, and prepared to sacrifice his evening on the altar of true friendship.

But it wasn't as much of a sacrifice as he had expected, talking to Tallia. Not only did she have all the intellect Jake had assumed she must have, she had personality astounding in someone who had seemed awkward and shy at first. The wine helped, of course. Jake was a master at getting wine into an unsuspecting woman, and he knew Tallia had no idea how much she was drinking; the trick was just to keep pouring tiny little amounts into her glass every time she took a sip. If she saw, she could hardly complain about such a piddling amount, and if she didn't see, so much the better.

An hour and a half into the evening the yellow legal pad was covered in notes about the liability coverage the gym would need before installing her Virtual Reality Holiday system, which was now very close to reality. Tallia and Jake were laughing together like old friends, Jake enjoying himself hugely. Brad, extremely annoyed, was sending Jake narrow-eyed messages, but Jake only shrugged with his eyebrows, as if he couldn't figure out himself why the phone call hadn't come.

Tallia was enjoying herself. Jake Drummond was exactly the kind of man who made her life a misery in her ordinary life, talking to her breasts even if he looked straight into her eyes, and it was a real pleasure to be treated like a human being by a man like him. Also, talking to Jake, who was sitting beside her, meant she could turn slightly away from Brad, and reduce the chance that during the evening he would suddenly recognize her. If he only saw the side view of Tallia, he might not be so quick to connect it with the front view of Natasha.

There was also the fact that she didn't have to be quite

so guarded as Tallia. It was Natasha whose personality, voice and mannerisms were put on. Tonight Tallia could basically be herself. So when she felt the effects of the wine, she didn't worry too much.

She couldn't figure out why Brad was looking like Chief Thundercloud, though.

The only thing Tallia didn't really enjoy was the actual food. Her teeth were fixed pretty firmly, but she wasn't going to take risks with food that needed any biting, or much chewing. So she chose vichyssoise, followed by lemon sole with rice. There had been little variation in texture and colour, and although the restaurant was good, even the flavours, taken all together, had seemed bland. Nothing contributed so much to altering her appearance as the overbite the false teeth gave her, Tallia reflected; they affected everything from the shape of her lower face to the way her voice sounded, but they were irritating. If she'd been Tallia, she'd have had them fixed ages ago.

No, wait a minute, what she meant was...

As the dessert menus arrived, Jake ripped the pages off the legal pad and slipped them, his pen and the pad into his briefcase, at the same time turning his phone back on. A few minutes later, as he knew it would, it rang. He had told one of the articling clerks working at the office tonight to try his number every twenty minutes till he got an answer.

"Right, right," he said, in response to an imagined tale of woe. "Yeah, I'd better come down. I'll see you in twenty minutes. Don't do anything before I get there.

"Sorry, Tallia, Brad, I've got to go," he said when he'd disconnected.

"I'm sorry to hear that," Brad said dangerously. He

had not missed the fact that the phone rang after Jake had gone into his briefcase again.

"There's a problem at the office I'll have to sort out. Tallia, great meeting you. I'm sure we'll meet again soon."

"What for?" Brad couldn't help saying, though he really didn't know why he was so pissed off with his friend, or suspected him of double-dealing. In all his life, Jake Drummond had never looked twice at a woman like Tallia Venables, and even if he had, was Brad jealous? He couldn't be, but still he said, "You seem to have covered everything pretty comprehensively. No reason for you to meet again."

Jake only grinned, and with a nod and a wink was gone.

"Your friend is very funny," Tallia told him.

Brad glowered. "I thought you said you didn't date."

Tallia blinked in astonishment. "But this wasn't a date, this was business," she pointed out.

"What Jake was talking about when he left was a date!" Brad said irritably. "I would have thought after your experiences with your research supervisor, you'd recognize the type!"

She opened her mouth in amazement at him. "Jake Drummond is nothing like Henry Clubbins! Are you crazy?"

Maybe he was. He sure didn't feel exactly sane. He had no idea why he suddenly felt possessive of Tallia. Maybe just a purely territorial response, he told himself.

"Jake goes through women a lot faster than he goes through cars."

"Beautiful women," Tallia said. "Correct me if I'm wrong."

"You could be a very attractive woman and you know

it,'' Brad said, wondering how the hell they had got to this point so fast. ''Do you think Jake isn't experienced enough to see through a disguise like this?''

Tallia nearly fainted. The room actually reeled for a moment. ''D-disguise?''

Oh well, he was in it now. He said, ''I don't know whether it was your experience with Clubbins or something earlier, maybe it was a whole string of unpleasant things, Tallia, but do you really think you're dealing with it in the best way?''

Tallia recovered her equilibrium, but the danger was far from over. It might be a very short step from thinking of her as in disguise to discovering who she was under that disguise. ''I'm afraid you have to leave that up to me, Brad. I'm dealing with life in my own way, and I'm sorry, but it's my own business.''

''Someday it might also be someone else's business.''

''I don't see that.''

''Suppose someone…got interested in you?'' Brad said awkwardly, not wanting to use those dangerous words, *fell in love with you*.

Tallia swallowed. Where on earth was this heading? Why was he so interested in the emotional life of an ugly duckling? Having been on the receiving end of attention almost entirely devoted to her looks for most of her adult life, to be actually liked *for herself* was such a new experience she couldn't recognize it.

She dropped her eyes and stirred her coffee unnecessarily. ''Well, if he's interested in me for who I am, why should I change?''

Good point, Brad realized. Good point. He really could not put his finger on the anomaly, though there was something buzzing around his brain. He wished it would settle on some surface so he could examine it.

Something about whether taking off a disguise constituted *change*.

"Okay," he said. "But you could be an attractive
woman as well as having the brains of the century, and
the combination would make you very, very formida-
ble."

Tallia laughed in genuine amusement. "Let me tell
you a secret. Men see either beauty or brains in a
woman, and if they see the former, they are blind to the
latter. You try talking intelligently to someone who
thinks you have the IQ of a carpet."

Brad stared at her. "Is *that* why —?" He broke off.

Her brown eyes gazed at him from behind the ugly
glasses. He thought absently that the frames completely
distorted the shape of her face. "Brad, you're assuming
a lot of things that haven't been proven. I suppose you
mean it as a compliment when you say I'm not making
enough of myself, but it's a little hard to take it as one."

She was right. What kind of idiot was he, taking a
woman out to dinner and as good as telling her he didn't
like the way she dressed and made up?

"Sorry," he said, shaking his head. "I guess that
counts as pretty ungentlemanly behaviour."

After that Tallia looked at her watch and said she
wanted an early night, and five minutes later they were
in the car. Brad rolled down the windows again. "Shall
we detour along the bay?" he asked. "It's a great
night."

Instinct told Tallia that she was in most danger of
being discovered when in darkness. The essence of a
person was much more likely to transmit to the other
person's receptors when they weren't getting visual information. "No, I'm tired after today," she said hastily.
"I'd like to get home, please."

It was a lie, and not easy to deliver. She liked being in Brad's company, and part of her was almost yearning for a repeat of that seawall walk.

Maybe she could risk it as Natasha, if he asked her again, she told herself sadly, and watched as Brad obediently took the direct route to her home.

"You have to stop dating him as Natasha," Bel said firmly. "It's just too dangerous, Tallia."

"I can't. I gave him my word for five dates, and we've only had one."

"Damon will have to give the money back."

"Stop talking like a logic quiz. This is human beings."

"Then you've got to tell him now, before you get in any deeper."

"I think I'm in too deep already. I will tell him, but first I want to get this stuff going into Fitness Now so that he'll think twice about cancelling my funding. He can't dump me if we're in the middle of installation."

"Big sister, for a girl with brains, you sure are acting stupid."

Part of her recognized the truth in that, but another part of her was terrified that a confession even now would mean neither of her would ever see Brad Slinger again. After a short struggle, that part won out.

"Bel, what I really need from you is advice on how to prevent him making the connection."

Bel sighed and gave up the attempt to make her sister see sense. It was as plain as plain that if she kept this up, the day was going to come when Brad would see through her disguises, but she was clearly not going to convince Tallia to forestall that awful moment. "Well, you're the actress, not me. What can you do to make your two alter egos more different than they are?''

''You're right. I have to make Natasha more…''

''Dumb may be the word you're searching for.''

''Yes, that too, but I think…more mannered. I have to give her little things that I never do as Tallia. Wrinkle her nose or give her a funny little shake of her head, or…''

''I guess you already wear two different perfumes,'' said the ever-practical Bel.

''I haven't been wearing any as Tallia.''

''Maybe you should. Smell is a big subconscious indicator, and you should disguise your own natural smell in both of you. If he ever smelled Natasha with her perfume worn off she'd smell just like Tallia.''

Tallia's eyes widened, ''Oh, wow, you're absolutely right! Something really light and floral, maybe.''

''And cheap. Expensive perfumes have a smell all their own.''

''Where would Ah be without you, little sister?'' said Natasha Fox with a winning smile. ''And there's one other thing that would be really convincing. I would need your help with that.''

''What?''

''He needs to see both of me at the same time. That would clinch it.''

7

"Barbeque?" stammered Natasha.

"At my cottage," Brad expanded glibly, just as if it were a sudden inspiration and not a critical step in his Get Natasha campaign. A casual, relaxed atmosphere, he told himself, and a live close-up of Natasha's legs in those Honey Childe cut-offs...he'd be able to make her relax her rules, he was sure. "We can swim and eat and then I'll bring you back home."

In a pig's eye I'll bring you back home, he promised himself silently.

"Oh, Ah...Ah don't think Ah could—" Tallia babbled, groping wildly for a way out. Cottage? Cottage meant swimsuits and no makeup and wet hair. "Actually, Ah forgot, can you believe it? It's staring at me raht heah in mah calendar, Ah have an appointment...." Her accent was getting thicker by the moment, but Brad didn't notice.

"Sunday, then," Brad said inexorably. Ha, he told himself jubilantly, he must be on the right track. That panic in her voice could only mean that she knew she'd be vulnerable in a casual situation.

If she said no, he'd just put it off till next weekend, Tallia thought miserably. If only she'd been quick enough, when he first suggested an afternoon date, to say that the deal was for evenings only. But she supposed it was too late for that now. She had to avoid any behaviour that might make him suspicious.

"All raht, Sunday," she said. "What if it rains?"

"We'll do something else. But it won't rain."

"You all tellin' me y'all got controllin' interest in the Divine now?"

"No, but I have great faith in the weather forecast."

Tallia prayed for rain. Natasha prayed for rain. Bel didn't bother. "Plan for the worst," Bel advised practically. "Praying's all right, but what are you going to wear if the answer's no?"

Brad pulled up not far from the building just as Tallia Venables came out the front door and walked down the street away from him. She didn't see him, and he heaved a sigh of relief. It wasn't the first time that the thought had occurred to him that trying to date two women who lived in the same building might be a tactical problem, but it made him see that he really had to do something about it.

"Ah'll be raht down," Natasha carolled in her breathy voice when he buzzed, and Brad, well-versed in the time perception of beautiful women, went back to the Porsche and settled down to wait. He was listening to the radio when he suddenly saw Tallia returning, but she was running up the steps before he had time to react, and didn't hear him call hello. Probably that was just as well, because just then Natasha came tripping down the steps past her. Of course the two women would have to know about each other, but he would prefer to make the announcement in his own time. He had no taste for awkward confrontations.

He eyed Natasha, as she approached, in some disappointment. She certainly wasn't looking like Honey Childe today. More like Jayne Mansfield in a 1950s film about Cannes. Smart cotton trousers, a big straw hat with floaty ties, jewelled sunglasses, a straw bag, and high-heeled sandals gave him some idea of the kind of summer cottage she was expecting. Brad, who hadn't bothered to shave, and was in worn shorts and T-shirt, with bare feet in leather Top-Siders, felt he'd wandered into the wrong movie. Oh, well, at least the car was right.

She fluttered across the road towards him in a manner that was completely unlike the part she'd played in the movie, and he wished that it were the other way around—that she'd been fluttery in the movie and natural and home-grown in real life. He got out and opened the door for her, and her heady perfume wafted over him. It struck him as particularly inappropriate for a summer day—the insects would love it—but he was pretty sure she considered it her signature scent or something, because it was the same one she wore at night.

"Hi!" she breathed, smiling broadly. "Isn't it just a wonderful day?"

The whispery voice wasn't entirely put on. Tallia was absolutely breathless with nerves. She had been terrified that Brad would be too quick for Bel, seeing her before he was meant to and coming over to talk to her or something. By the time the two sisters had passed each other Tallia had been practically at heart-attack pitch, but Bel, cool as a pond on a spring day and looking remarkably like Tallia in the outfit, had just winked at her and grabbed the door Tallia was holding for her. Tallia only started breathing normally again when the door closed and she was on the pavement, and saw Brad still in the car.

"Do you know Tallia Venables?" Brad asked, as he

let in the clutch, thinking this was as good an opportunity as any.

Natasha wrinkled her nose attractively. "Ah don't think so. Who is she?"

"You just passed her. She lives in your building."

"Oh! Do you mean that weird scientist woman on the fourth floor?"

"Is she weird?" Brad asked peaceably.

"Well, she surely isn't very attractive, is she?" she said, aiming for a bitchy note.

"I guess not. She's extremely intelligent, however."

Natasha turned wide black sunglasses his way. "Do y'all know her?"

"She's an inventor, as you say. I thought I should tell you I date her, in case the subject ever comes up."

"You date her?" Natasha repeated, her voice a mixture of horror and astonishment that did Brad's heart a peck of good. So she could be jealous, even while keeping him at arm's length. He repressed a smile. "You do—"

Tallia heard what she had nearly said—*you do not date her!*—and abruptly broke off. Natasha could hardly know the facts. But *date her?* One business dinner with his lawyer! What was his reason for such a stupid lie? Trying to make her jealous? Well, she'd show him! As if she'd be jealous of such a...

Brad glanced at her curiously. "Yeah, why not?"

"She's got an overbite!"

Wait a minute, wait a minute. Tallia pulled herself up short. This was herself she was getting steamed about. Boy oh boy, this charade was going to drive her nuts, if she didn't watch it.

Brad laughed. "It's not her teeth I'm investing in." *Not yet,* he told himself.

"Investing! Ah thought y'all said you were dating her, like a girlfriend. Or is she under contract, same as me? She gets investment money if she'll date you?"

"This is very flattering to my ego. It might surprise you to know that I do not normally have to bribe women to date me. Some are even quite flattered by my interest," Brad said.

Well, she could appreciate that. "Just me and this Tallia, huh? So why are y'all bribing us if there are so many more fish in the sea?"

"I am not paying Tallia Venables to date me," Brad said stiffly.

"Do y'all kiss her?" Natasha asked, wondering just how far this lie would take him, and what reason he could have.

"Not yet," Brad said cheerfully.

Tallia abruptly lost her grip on Natasha, and went shivery over her whole body at the thought that Brad was contemplating kissing her in spite of her teeth, skin, hair and clothes. Her next thought was despair that she should finally have found a man who liked her for her brain, and she had made it impossible for him ever to do anything about it. She could not kiss him as the Tallia he knew. Natasha might kiss him, but it was the Natasha part of her whom men had kissed all her adult life, the Tallia who had never been kissed.

It almost broke her heart. If she could think of a way out of this stupid scam she was running…

"Why are y'all telling me about it?"

Brad clocked the depression in her voice. He had been almost certain she was attracted to him, but this kind of jealousy he had not expected. He wondered how long it would be before she cracked.

"Because I'm dating you and I want you to know that it's not an exclusive arrangement."

"What is it? Some kind of beauty-brains thing? Trying to make up your mind what you want most?" Tallia was surprised by the thought she voiced. It really did sometimes seem as though, in the effort to become Natasha, she contacted another part of herself altogether, with strengths she knew nothing about.

It was certainly close enough to make him look at her with respect. Natasha might not have intellect, Brad told himself, but she had good gut instincts where human relations were concerned. This wasn't the first time he'd noticed that.

"I guess something like that."

"Y'all got a bet on, or something?"

Now, this really startled him. How in the hell had she guessed that? He'd have denied it under torture, though, because torture was what he knew he'd be in for if either of them found out about Jake's dare.

"Of course not!" he said, coldly indignant.

"Well, sorry, but a man who's willing to throw a quarter of a million dollars at a woman for five dates—and all the time he's also dating someone else! It does kind of stick out, doesn't it?"

That was unanswerable. He fell back on, "Does it?"

She was mentally kicking herself. Natasha was supposed to bore him with her lack of brains, not impress him with her psychological insight. She wanted to be as different as possible from Tallia.

"Oh, Ah don't know." Natasha shrugged. "Look, y'all can date who you want, there's no reason to tell me anything about it. Ah'm under contract to you as much as Tallia is, after all. We've got three more dates after this, you and me, and then we're history."

Only if I've got you out of my system by then, Brad warned her silently.

The cottage was not at all what she had expected. Not a rich man's summer home at all, it was a log cabin, genuinely rough, the kitchen and bathroom both primitive, the place solid but unadorned by the polished pine floors and casually smart kelims she had imagined. It was one large room with a fireplace and three small rooms and the bathroom off. The furniture, except for a couple of battered sofas, looked as though someone had hammered it together out of spare timber or logs as it was needed.

The cabin sat on its own private lake, surrounded by forest. There was a canoe in a shed, a rough wooden pier, a small fishing boat drawn up onshore beside it. The beach was grassy, and then sand and stones led into sparkling, clear water.

Tallia would have given her eyeteeth to be able strip off and jump in. But Natasha had to pretend a horror of the sun and distaste for the water and refuse to swim. Brad didn't try to override her, but stripped down to a neat pair of trunks not designed to draw attention to his masculine equipment—something else that surprised her—and went in like a seal to his natural home.

In the end, she couldn't resist. Natasha, her hair tucked up, hat and sunglasses undisturbed, did a few minutes of the breast stroke, while Brad, watching, silently promised himself to dismantle that ridiculous poise one of these days. A woman that beautiful had no business worrying about her looks, because she'd still be beautiful half drowned.

Or would she? For the first time, Brad found himself wondering just how much of Natasha's face would come off if he put her under the pump and gave her a brisk scrub. He supposed she would consider that a violation of his promise, but he sure would love to do it. He wanted to see the natural woman.

The thought of it was enough to make him hard. Well, the thought and the sight of Natasha coming up out of the water in her neat two-piece, the water glistening off her high breasts, firm muscles and flawless skin...

If he'd thought he'd seen a flash of intelligence, though, either he was mistaken or the flash didn't happen often. Natasha was resolutely dumb and self-centred all the rest of the afternoon. She would gaze at him and pretend to listen with wide-eyed interest, and then say something that only proved her thoughts hadn't been following his at all.

She asked him about his Fitness Now chain, and he answered briefly, not wanting to get into a business frame of mind today, but he soon saw how little he needed to worry about that. Natasha listened to him with an air of really breathless fascination, and then said with a certain satisfaction, "*Ah* work out regularly. But Ah never overdo it. A woman shouldn't have hard muscles, really, should she?"

The sun and water and relaxation and her presence were making Brad feel pretty sexy, and he could have said something there, but he restrained himself. She was certainly playing some kind of game, he could see that now, and he wasn't going to call her bluff till he knew what it was. He wondered whether the whole thing had been cooked up between her and Damon Picton as a deliberate means of extorting money from him. He'd heard that they'd once been engaged, and since then neither had married...maybe they were still involved secretly. Well, he would find out in time.

Natasha kept her straw hat on all day, even when she helped him barbecue the meal. They had saved it till about seven, when the sun was dropping behind the tree-tipped hill, and a little breeze was flicking over the lake.

It was the breeze that was her undoing. It caught at the floppy brim of her hat, and Natasha instinctively grabbed at it. In doing so, she banged her hand against a hot utensil. She yelped in pain, leaping back to avoid the utensil as it fell to the ground, her wrist in her mouth in the instinctive response of the burned.

Brad quickly tipped up one of their drinks and pressed an ice cube against the place, but even so, there was a dark red burn across the back of her hand that had gone several layers deep. Brad had a first aid kit in the kitchen, and he soothed the burn with some ointment and wrapped it with gauze. It was only as he firmly turned her hand to fasten the bandage with some adhesive tape that either of them realized that he was touching her.

It was the fact that touch had been forbidden between them, no doubt, that caused them both to be so electrified with awareness. Natasha's face went pink, and the blood in Brad's body got similarly localized, and they stared at each other for five long seconds, Brad at her face, Natasha at Brad's thighs.

He couldn't believe he was hard just touching her wrist. She couldn't believe how riveting an erection in a bathing suit could be. At last she pulled her gaze away, only to run into the heat of his eyes on her.

He said nothing, only silently willed her to give him the word that would release him from his promise. He bent his head, his mouth coming closer to hers, to encourage her. One word would be enough. He hovered there, a few inches from a kiss, feeling the blood hammer in his body and in her pulse, knowing that she wanted what he wanted.

Tallia couldn't speak. She knew that if she did, she would say exactly the wrong thing. She must not say *kiss me* or *yes* or even *oh, Brad!* But they were the only words she could think of. So she licked her lips, swallowed, and was resolutely silent. His mouth got closer.

Brad's hand had unconsciously tightened on her arm, and now he lifted his other hand towards her hair. "Natasha, say it," he breathed.

It was the hand moving towards her hair that released her from her hypnotic trance. Her hair that was a wig. Instinct told her that Brad would not be a gentle lover, the kind who leaves his partner's hair untousled. If Brad made love to a woman, she would come out of the experience with every cell disturbed, she was sure. His hands would be in her hair and everywhere else over her body....

"Brad, you promised," Tallia managed to whisper. She shivered and drew her hand from his hold, and turned away.

They sat down to eat on opposite sides of the round cedar table, but distance didn't help much. All her rejection had done was heighten their awareness, and the succulent steaks and the buttery, crunchy charcoal-baked potatoes didn't do anything to lessen their appetite for each other.

Especially as Brad couldn't take his eyes off her through the whole meal. She didn't think it was deliberate, but every time he put a morsel of food in his mouth, gazing at her, she felt as if he was saying he'd rather be kissing her, licking her...she tried to look away, but his eyes were just like a magnet, and kept drawing hers.

His voice had gone all gravelly, too, so whenever he spoke he seemed to be stroking her. If it was deliberate, he was very, very practised, Tallia warned herself, and she was probably lucky that circumstances were preventing her from giving in. Probably a woman could get really stuck on a man who could do this to her senses. She was pretty sure *she* could, even if it didn't hold true for womanhood as a whole. She knew it would be stupid to set her heart on a man like Brad Slinger. Suppose when he made love to her she fell for him completely? She could really believe a thing like that could happen, that you could get physically addicted to the kind of pleasure he seemed to be promising to give her.

She believed the silent promise. There was just something about Brad—not least the fact that he never said it in words. She'd had her share of men promising to drive her crazy in bed, but somehow all that talk just seemed to be hot air. She was always convinced that it was their own pleasure they were really thinking about.

Brad never said it. But he kept looking at her as if he was figuring out what she might like when she did crack. *Sensitive there,* she saw him marking her with his eyes, *there, maybe there.* She'd never felt this from a man before, and it wasn't easy to resist, not with her heart leaping around like a lab frog in her chest every time his eyes made electric contact with hers.

"Wig," she said once, to remind herself, not meaning to say it aloud. Not realizing she had said it aloud till she heard her own voice, sounding almost desperate.

He was talking about cooking, about rubbing olive oil and salt into a potato before wrapping it in corn leaves and shoving it into the hot coals, but the only words really making any impact on either of them were words like "oil" and "rub" and "skin" and "hot."

"What?" Brad said, surfacing with a start and blinking at her.

"Wig—ot to go soon," Tallia invented wildly. "What time is the last ferry?"

Damn, Brad thought, glancing at his watch. Who'd have thought such a candy-floss-looking woman would turn out to be the Iron Lady? He'd never encountered such resistance. Maybe he was losing his touch. Or maybe he just wanted her too much and his desperation was putting her off. He'd heard that it did, but he hadn't been this desperate for a woman since he was eighteen and sex was life.

"Just over an hour," he told her. She had the self-preservation instincts of a cat. How had she known he was planning to miss the last ferry by two minutes? He was beginning to revise his definition of what constituted intelligence. She might not be able to add two and two, but she had some other way of knowing things.

Tallia jumped up. "We'd better move, then. We have some cleaning up to do, haven't we?"

So the best-laid plans of mice and men went up the spout yet again.

8

The next morning Tallia gazed at the angry red burn across the back of her hand in deep dismay. Whatever she did about bandaging it, whatever she wore, it would be noticeable.

And she was due to meet Brad at a Fitness Now today, to look over the premises.

How was Tallia Venables going to explain a scar in the same place where Natasha had burned herself?

"Pretty clumsy," Bel observed. "What was Natasha doing helping with the cooking, anyway? I thought we decided she was going to be the brainless, useless, self-centred flower type so he'd lose his hots for her?"

"I forgot," Tallia muttered. "I kind of slipped into Honey Childe without thinking. She's earthy and casual."

Bel rolled her eyes. "Well, that is unmistakably a burn, and unless you're thinking of dressing in a medieval dress with pointed sleeves you can't risk seeing him today."

"I was thinking maybe I could just put some elastoplast on it and say I gave blood."

"Yeah, like they really take a pint of blood from the back of your hand," Bel said.

"Don't they?"

"Tal, your vein would collapse!"

"There must be something I can do!"

"A nice little dose of summer flu is what you can do."

"But this is so important! We're discussing the installation today!"

"My heart bleeds for you," said Bel with what Tallia considered extreme lack of feeling. "If you want to keep the lab, you should not let Brad Slinger make the discovery for himself that you are playing games with him. Therefore you will have to sacrifice today's pleasures for the guarantee of future ones."

Tallia shuddered. "Oh, God, how did I get into this?"

"The same way you've got into trouble all your life," said her ruthless little sister. "You backed into it. If you go into something without looking where you're going, you shouldn't be surprised if when you turn around you're in the room with a monster."

So Tallia rang the lab to tell her assistant she was in bed with a summer cold. She didn't ring Brad at all, partly as punishment for his lies about her to Natasha yesterday. Date him? Let him see that if her calendar wasn't right there in front of her eyes she forgot all about a meeting with him.

Backing into trouble, as Bel said.

At one o'clock there was a hammering at her door, and then she heard the sound of Bel's key in the lock. "Tal!" her sister screamed, tearing into the kitchen. "Thank God you're here! Brad phoned! He's coming around to see you!"

The next five minutes were an insane mixture of rushing around and listening to babbled explanations that Tal hoped she would never experience again as long as she lived. "He thought I was you!" Bel panted, patting on the foundation makeup, making Tal's nose red, and pulling on her drab brown wig, while Tal clipped in her overbite and painted on her dark eyebrows. "The phone rang, and when I answered he naturally thought I was you." It was not unusual for the sisters to be mistaken for each other on the phone, even by members of their own family. "And if I wasn't you, Tal, who was I? I just couldn't think!"

So she had pretended to be Tallia, and Brad had announced he was coming around to visit her sickbed and hung up before she had the chance to protest.

"Where's that thing you bind your chest with?"

Between them, they turned her into Tallia the frump in record time, and then Bel, carefully looking into the corridor first in case Brad had been let in downstairs, made a dash for the stairs and back to her own apartment.

Tallia put her duvet and pillow on the sofa and practised looking sick. It helped that the day was grey and rainy, and the light coming into the room washed her out, but she was more nervous than she'd ever been playing this part. Her terry bathrobe had cuffs, which she had unrolled to hide the strip of elastoplast on her hand, but she must try to keep the hand hidden. She was feeling anything but confident and leapt guiltily to her feet when Brad rang the buzzer.

"Brad, I really am feeling too sick to want company," she said down the entryphone, but he said masterfully, "I won't stay long."

If she had really been ill, she might have refused to let him in, but there's nothing like guilt to confuse natural behaviour, and Tallia was frightened about what he might imagine if she stuck to her guns. Two minutes later, he came through the door.

"Brad, what are you doing here?" she asked feebly.

He had flowers in his hand, and he carried them across the room and offered them to her. She took them awkwardly, with one hand.

"Thank you, they're lovely," said Tallia, sniffing them. "But you'll catch my bug." She didn't dare get up to put them in water, he might see her hand. So she left them lying on the duvet.

"I never catch bugs. How are you feeling?"

She sniffed. She had put drops in her eyes to make her nose run. "Not very bad, I'll be back in the lab in a day or two."

"Have you eaten anything? Shall I get you some soup?"

"You're a great cook, Brad, but I really don't need anything, thanks."

Brad wrinkled his brow in smiling curiosity. "Now, what makes you think I can cook?"

All her face muscles seemed to congeal. It was Natasha who had discovered that Brad could cook. And only yesterday.

Brad knew he hadn't told Tallia, because unless he cooked for them, people didn't know. The only one he'd cooked for lately was Natasha. Brad tilted his head.

"Do you know Natasha Fox?" he asked.

If she said no, how could she explain what she knew? She looked at him in righteous wrath. "You told her we were dating!" she said, using the chance to sidetrack the discussion. "You told her you were bribing me with research funding!"

Brad wanted to kick himself. Suddenly the explanation for her sudden "flu" seemed obvious. For a man who thought he knew women he sure was screwing up a lot lately! "She jumped to conclusions. She was jealous," he added desperately, when that didn't seem to soothe her.

"*Jealous?*" Tallia screeched, outraged. She had *not* been jealous!

Brad shook his head. Boy, was he messing this up! He hadn't realized just how paranoid Tallia was around the subject of men.

Oh, boy, was she messing this up! Tallia thought desperately. Why should Tallia be angry at the suggestion that Natasha was jealous?

"Why shouldn't she be jealous of you?" he asked. "She's not as intelligent as you are."

"She's not intelligent enough to be jealous about it, either," she said ungraciously.

"She doesn't have your kind of brain, but she is by no means stupid." Breaking all the rules, Brad, he told himself irritably, praising one woman to another. "How well do you know her?"

Tallia was pretty sure Natasha had told him that they'd only met in the corridors. She should be writing notes after every encounter. "She came up last night on some pretext to check out the competition. I was very surprised to hear that I *was* the competition."

He looked right into her eyes in a way that made her heart pound. "You can't go on hiding forever, Tallia."

Suddenly her mouth was bone dry, and the little Marlon Brando pads that puffed out her lower jaw went fuzzy, sending shivers along her spine and nerves. Her lips wouldn't move over her false teeth. Tallia tore her gaze from his, and struggled to sit upright.

The flowers slipped and she grabbed at them, and then she felt the worst happening—her breast flattener gently gave way and slipped down to her waist in one smooth movement. Her breasts burst free behind the light cotton of her nightgown just as the duvet slid away from them. Tallia abandoned the flowers to their fate and snatched at her robe with her good hand, trying to pull it closed.

Too late. Brad was staring. At breasts where breasts had not been before. "Tallia," he said. "What the heck has happened to you?"

"It's a new invention!" she lied wildly. "I've been experimenting on myself!"

"You've invented a breast developer that *works?* My God, you're a millionaire overnight. Will you sell me the exploitation rights?"

"There are a lot of wrinkles to iron out, Brad. It might be dangerous."

She couldn't believe where this conversation was going. She'd never felt so out of control in her life.

"Is it a drug? You shouldn't be experimenting on yourself with drugs!" he said with sudden worry.

"No, no, it's a—it's a—I can't tell you about it yet, Brad," Tallia said frantically. "I'm not sure whether the effects will last, or what."

"Is this why you called in sick today?"

"Yes—no, Brad, I wish you'd leave now."

"Are you already in a deal with someone else? Is that the problem?"

"No, no!" she assured him hastily. "If it works, you're the first—but I'm not sure..." She trailed off, miserably aware of how stupid she sounded.

Brad looked at her with a slow smile. He was pretty sure he understood now. But whatever her psychological problems were, he didn't see that it would gain anything for him to pretend. "Look, Tallia, it's not going to make all that much difference. Whether you like it or not, you've got a funny kind of attraction all your own, with or without breasts. There's just something about you that men like.''

She gazed up at him. ''Including you?''

''Including me.'' *And Jake,* he could have told her, but he wasn't going to plead Jake's case for him before he was sure what his own was.

''Oh, *no!*'' Tallia wailed involuntarily. How had she gotten herself into the position where a man was telling her he liked her for herself and she couldn't take him up on it?

''Please don't panic, Tallia. I'm not going to jump you, and I'm not going to try to buy you.'' In fact, he was feeling protective of her, and that wasn't a feeling that assailed him often. ''But you may as well know that your efforts to tone down your physical attractiveness don't hide the essential you.''

''You think men are attracted to the essential me?'' Tallia asked bitterly.

''Any man worth worrying about, yes.''

''What about Natasha Fox? Are men attracted to the inner woman there, too?''

Brad grinned. So she was jealous. ''It's harder to see past such obvious beauty, I admit. But don't think that Natasha is all looks. When she lets herself go, she's not nearly so self-obsessed as she seems at first, and she's got a gut intelligence that even you shouldn't sneer at. She understands people.''

Tallia could have wept. She'd finally found what she'd been looking for all her life—a man who could see past the surface. And she just couldn't think of any way to tell him the truth about her without losing him.

* * *

"We have to think of something!" she told Bel desperately. "Help me think!"

Bel had returned to her apartment as soon as Tal phoned that the coast was clear. Now she was sprawled on a few cushions on the floor. "Funny, isn't it, that you never listen to my advice before you get into trouble, but always want my advice for getting out of it?" she observed mildly, pulling a bit of fluff off her inside-out sweatshirt.

"Yes, but never mind that now!" Tallia said, forbearing to point out that the plain disguise had been Bel's idea from the start. "What can I do? Can I confess now?"

"Sure you can confess now."

"Really? You think—"

"...if you don't care about your lab funding or ever seeing Brad Slinger again," Bel said dryly. "Of course you can't confess now! What, just at the moment when he's not sure which of you he wants, you're going to take a step that will convince him he doesn't want either of you?"

All the breath left Tallia in a dejected whoosh. "You're right. I can't tell him. So what can I do?"

"You have to play for time, I guess."

"What good is time going to do me?"

Bel's forefingers went up in a sudden characteristic gesture. "Wait a minute, wait a minute, I've got an idea."

Tallia, who, brainy as she was, had always accepted that Bel was the real genius in the family, watched her sister anxiously. Bel started nodding to herself, then pushed her hair back behind her ears. "Right. The trick is to get him involved emotionally so that when he does find out, he can't actually walk away, don't you think?"

Tallia frowned dubiously. "Don't you think that the more emotionally involved he was, the more hurt or upset or angry or something he'd be?"

"Yeah, but he'd still have to come back if he loved you, right? Not so easy to walk away from love."

The word *love* made Tallia go all goose-bumpy. Was Bel right? Might he fall in love with one of her? Suddenly she understood how much she would want that to happen. Her eyes widened as she realized that maybe losing the lab wouldn't be the worst thing that could happen to her as a result of her deceit.

"Oh, Bel, I'm afraid!"

"No, no, we can do this! What we have to do is slowly bring your two alter egos together."

"What?"

Still thinking furiously, Bel said, "Yeah—like, Natasha gets smart, or Tallia gets beautiful. Then the other one disappears."

"Disappears?" Tallia repeated blankly. She had never felt so stupid in her life.

"Out of his life. Which one do you want him to fall in love with?"

"I don't believe he'll fall in love with either of me. Not after the way he's been—he's sure to think I've deliberately played him for a sucker! Can't I just confess, Bel?"

Her sister regarded her levelly. "If you tell him now, both of you will lose him." She sounded just like an oracle. Tallia shivered.

"Okay." She pressed her hands to her eyes.

"What you have to decide is who you want him to really fall for, Tallia or Natasha."

"You think the choice is mine?"

"He's already told you that he thinks Tallia's attractive and Natasha's smart! A man doesn't start seeing those hidden depths in a woman unless he's falling for her, if ever. So, who do you want it to be?''

"Tallia, I guess," Tallia said, her head buzzing with confusion. "I mean, that's the person I am and want to be. But Brad's much more attracted to Natasha."

"Never mind what Brad wants—he's going to have both of you in the end, after all! So, we embark on the Make Tallia Beautiful campaign. You've made a great start there with the breasts already."

"What do you mean—*keep* them? I was going to tell him the effect didn't last."

"No, you can't do that! It's too good an opportunity."

"But he'll want to patent the technique! He says I can make millions from it."

Bel waved her hand. "You just have to convince him the market testing would be too risky. And you have to get braces on your teeth right away."

"The process takes years! Are you saying I can't—"

"Tal, you won't have to wait years to have straight teeth again. All you have to do right now is make him think you're going to be beautiful, so that he chooses you over Natasha, that's all. Don't forget at the end of all this you're going to confess. You can take your teeth off then. Meanwhile, start talking about how you might be going to dye your hair."

"To *Brad?* Why would I talk to him about something like that? No woman would."

"Oh, come on. Just talk the way a woman would who was testing the waters. 'Gee, I wonder what I'd look like if I coloured my hair blond?'" Bel mimicked, in a silly voice, bobbing her head.

"Yeah, but he's supposed to say, don't do it, I like

you just the way you are,'' Tallia pointed out firmly. ''What do I do if he says that?''

''Act flattered, tell him men don't understand these things, and then do it anyway, just the way any woman would. Now, on the Natasha side of things you've been slipping up. You aren't supposed to be making him admire you, Tal, you're supposed to be boring him.''

''I know. I couldn't help myself. It's kinda weird, you know, but before, I've been so determined to make people see how smart I am in spite of my looks that I always kind of avoided that dumb-but-intuitive-blonde thing. But when I'm not trying to prove anything, this other kind of gut logic just sort of happens.''

''What are you trying to say?''

''I don't know. Maybe that in one side of myself, I really am that person I've always insisted on not being—beautiful but dumb.''

''Nobody who'd seen you walk into this mess could doubt that, big sister,'' Bel told her, with every appearance of delight.

''I should never have started this,'' Brad was saying. ''I'm telling you, Jake, I'm falling for two women for something completely different in each of them.''

''I admit Tallia's brain is enough to make a man overlook a certain lack of physical attributes,'' Jake said grudgingly. He was sorry he'd ever gotten involved with this. Without his help Brad would probably have forgotten all about his intentions towards Tallia, but now it seemed as if Jake's interference was going to bring down on his friend the very fate he'd hoped to help him avoid. ''But think how much more easily Natasha's looks make up for lack of brain.''

''No, you see—that's just it! You don't get it.''

"What don't I get?" Jake asked patiently.

"It's Tallia I like for her looks, and Natasha I like for her brain."

There was a long, pregnant silence. "Okay, you have to run that by me again. It got away," said Jake.

"I know it doesn't make any sense. But...Tallia's as plain as a pastry, it's true, but there's just something about the way she moves—she's kind of unconsciously graceful in a way that Natasha just isn't. Natasha's so self-conscious about her beauty she almost makes herself not beautiful at all."

Jake rolled his eyes upward. "Sure."

"You've only seen her in that movie, and she was playing a part. If you were around her more, you'd see what I meant. I'm not saying I don't get the hots—around a body like that, who wouldn't? But the looks don't get to me on an emotional level. I mean, those mammoth breasts, they're like any man's fantasy until you really think about it. Tallia's breasts, on the other hand—of course, all that story she told me is a crock, she's just been flattening them to stop men being interested—they're sort of real, you know what I mean? I could live with breasts like that. When they practically burst out of her nightgown it was all I could do not to—" He paused for a moment, remembering.

"What I really *like* about Natasha is that kind of deep, intuitive, feminine mind she's got. She kind of looks right at you and then devastates you with some understanding of your real motives—it really shakes me up when that happens, Jake. It gets to me, know what I mean?"

"I haven't got the faintest idea, old buddy. But you

keep on talking, anyway. I'm sure it'll do you good, and I can always bill you for psychotherapeutic listening.''

"If I could just give Natasha Tallia's looks, or Tallia Natasha's brain," Brad sighed despairingly.

9

Under the influence of Bel's advice, Tallia decided that it would be best to get the five dates as Natasha over with before embarking on her beautify Tallia campaign. "And also," Bel suggested, "it wouldn't hurt to get him ready for Natasha's departure."

"What, you mean, start talking about suicide?" Tallia asked dryly. Something in her did not like what she was planning now, but the arguments against trying to solve her dilemma in a more direct way were pretty strong. She knew now that she did not want to risk losing Brad, and if she looked at it logically, Bel's solution probably stood the best chance of success.

"Ha ha," said Bel tolerantly. "You have to say you're going to be out of town shooting a film for an indefinite period and he should squeeze his dates in before—no, wait, I've got it!" Bel jumped up. "Oh, this is great, this is genius! It's staring us in the face!" She whirled to face Tallia.

"You tell him you're going to Hollywood to seek your fortune, of course!"

Tallia stared at her with deep misgiving. "I do?"

"Sure! What could be more logical than for Natasha Fox to want to try the big time? And then it'll be over, finito, done! You've left town!"

Tallia liked it. Bel was right, it was the perfect way to rush the dates and get Natasha out of Brad's life. And yet…

"His mother ran away from him to Hollywood," she told Bel tentatively. "You don't think—"

"What?"

"Oh, I don't know. I just—what if he does really like Natasha, the way you said? Won't he be hurt?"

"For a bright girl, you're pretty dumb sometimes," her sister informed her affectionately. "Don't you see? He's going to have Tallia!"

Brad looked across the table and wished he were not so aroused by a woman who was so determinedly All Woman. The length of Natasha's eyelashes was only exceeded by the length of her long, purple nails. Her breasts seemed to reach halfway across the table to him. She had so much hair her face seemed lost.

None of these attributes were things he'd ever valued in a woman, and it irritated the hell out of him to find that he was a pretty typical male after all. All the externals, and all of them might easily be false, but still the wanting to bed her was unmerciful. He couldn't believe it. It must be premature senility or something. Why didn't a woman as beautiful as this have any confidence in her beauty? Why didn't she just let it be? He couldn't figure it out.

"Now, let me see," she was saying. She was counting on her fingers, making a big play of the nails in a way that was feline without being graceful. He thought of the way Tallia moved her hands and figured she could give Natasha lessons in femininity. Tallia's motions were unselfconscious and more graceful than he'd ever seen in a woman. Natasha's conscious attempts at grace simply made her seem calculated. Didn't she ever relax?

"This is our third date, raht?"

And counting, Brad added. He was pretty sure by now that in spite of his reservations there was only going to be one way he could get Natasha out of his system. To that end he'd brought her to one of his favourite pre-seduction haunts, a grubby but wildly expensive little place only the cognoscenti knew about, that had a menu stuffed with known aphrodisiacs and a piano player who could melt marble.

"Kiss me again, rekiss and kiss me again," the singer was begging softly now, into a mike that was very close to his lips.

"Well, Ah should tell you that Ah'll be leavin' town in just under three weeks, so if you want those other two dates, it'll have to be before Ah go."

"Why not after you come back?"

She smiled broadly. "Well, if things go the way Ah hope, Ah won't be comin' back, that's why."

Brad frowned suddenly. "No? Where are you going?"

She took a deep excited breath, and her breasts nearly knocked her wine over. "Los Angeles!"

"Damn," Brad said softly.

Natasha blinked. "Pahn me?"

He shook his head. "I thought you said you weren't interested in going to Hollywood."

"Did Ah? Oh, goodness, that's right! Your stepfather!" She might be an actress, but she was no spy, Tallia reflected ruefully. As the full conversation of that night came back to her, she realized unhappily what she had to do to make this really believable. "Ah forgot all about him." She beamed at him, as if what she were saying was a lie.

He smiled grimly. Well, he had known. He had told himself the moment would come. He wasn't sure when he'd started hoping to be proved wrong about her, but it had been a damn stupid hope. "Of course," he said. "You'd like an introduction to Garth."

Hating herself, Tallia sighed and smiled. "Oh, Brad, could you? Would you?"

He thought suddenly, *I could make sex the price,* but he had never paid a woman for sex and he wasn't starting now, not even as a surefire way to get her out of his system. He figured nothing would put you off a woman faster than buying her, but if he couldn't get Natasha through natural seduction, he'd do without.

Always discounting the fact that he was paying fifty thousand dollars for her time right now. But he was sure she would consider that different. That was a sacrifice on the altar of Art.

"Sure, I'll call him tomorrow, tell him you're coming," he said. She was sweetly grateful, and he guessed tonight's efforts were going to be completely wasted. She might be willing, but he was damned if he'd make love to a grateful woman. Or at least, to a woman who was only giving in because she was grateful.

Tallia saw the light go out of his eyes and knew she should be glad. If he was no longer interested in Natasha, that made her job easier, didn't it? Yet somehow his loss of interest killed all her pleasure in the evening.

"Let me get this straight," Jake said. "You've got the perfect leverage and you're not going to use it?"

"Duty sex is not a thing I've ever listed among my must haves in this life," Brad said.

"No, but Natasha Fox is."

Brad made no response, and Jake eyed him as he took a drink. "You know what it is, Brad? It's pride. You're miffed that she hasn't fallen for your handsome masculinity, and you don't want to think it's your connections and not your handsome visage that has got her."

"Shut up," Brad said genially.

"You want her to like you for yourself!" Jake informed him with a broad grin.

Brad dug into his steak and pretended not to hear.

Jake shook his head and sucked in his breath. "I smell danger, boy, real danger! When a man starts wanting a woman to see the real man under all the money and influence—I hear wedding bells, Brad! And incidentally, I hear that I have won my bet."

"She's going to Hollywood, remember?"

Jake leaned over the table and spoke confidentially. "You know what? You could make her stay. If you asked, she'd stay."

"What makes you think so?"

"Call it what you like." His friend tapped his nose. "It wouldn't surprise me at all to know that this is a deliberate ploy to make you declare yourself, make you shape up and realize how you feel about her."

"Well, she's chosen the wrong man and the wrong game plan. I will not ask her to stay."

"No?"

"If she's got the itch, Jake, sooner or later it's going to get too strong for her. I don't want to be the father of her kids when that day comes. I'll cut my losses now, thanks."

"If you can," Jake said.

"He looked pretty unhappy," Tallia told her sister. "I kind of wish I'd said Europe or Toronto instead of Hollywood. I think the association was really painful for him.''

''Never mind. Don't forget someday he's going to know the truth. This is all just temporary, right?''

''I wish I hadn't started this. I wish there were another way out.''

''If you tell him now, before he's committed, Tal, the risk is too great. Just think of your lab when you start having doubts. How much you like having all that computer equipment to play with...''

Tallia toyed with the thought of telling Bel the truth—that the most important consideration was not that she should not lose her lab, but that she should not lose Brad. And that she had the awful feeling that she'd already done just that.

Things were progressing on the Virtual Reality front. Brad was now expanding one of his Fitness Now clubs, installing a small wave pool and having the walls of the room painted with trompe l'oeil images of South Sea scenes, preparatory to running a test programme of her invention. This entailed regular meetings between them, and Tallia grew more nervous with each one.

''So, Tallia, I see the effects of the breast enhancer are permanent,'' Brad joked one day, as they went over the details.

Tallia grinned sheepishly. ''Looks like it.''

''I'm glad you trust me more than you did. One day you might even leave off the wig, right?''

Tallia remembered Bel's advice. ''Who knows? I might even dye my hair blond!''

She was unprepared for the look that crossed his face, instantly suppressed. ''Oh, don't do that,'' he said easily.

He's in love with Natasha, she told herself bitterly. *When she goes, I've lost my chance.*

But there was nothing she could do about it. She could hardly kill off Tallia and become Natasha for the rest of her life.

"Will you have dinner with me tonight?" he asked.

"We're having lunch now," she pointed out nervously.

"We're having a business lunch. I'd like to take you out for a pleasure dinner," Brad said, with a smile that melted her.

"Oh, Brad!" she said nervously. Bel was right. She had to get Natasha out of the picture first, so that the chance of comparison was reduced. "I wish you wouldn't ask me just now!"

"I wish you'd tell me what it is that's made you afraid of me."

Tallia dropped her head. "I'm not afraid of you, Brad."

It was the truth, but it sounded like a lie. "Then come to dinner with me."

"Why do you want me to?" she said, her brown eyes looking at him in the direct way she had that was a little reminiscent of Natasha's blue gaze.

Good question. *Because I am almost sure that I am attracted to you on a deep level that no woman has ever disturbed before,* he might have said, *and if that is the case, I want to start making you more interested in me than you seem right now.* But he was afraid of her reaction if he made a clear declaration of interest.

"Tallia, not every man you meet is a potential rapist," he said instead.

She stared at him. Is that what he thought she was afraid of? That he was— How had she let that happen?

"Brad, I have never thought that you were a potential rapist!" she said emphatically.

"No?"

"Of course not! Never! Not even that night—" She broke off in confusion, because she was about to mention his first meeting with Natasha. *I want to kiss you,* he had said. She looked at him now and was despairingly sure she had missed her chance with him forever. Why hadn't she kissed him that night? Why—

"What night?" he asked in surprise.

"Never mind. I just never thought that about you, that's all."

"Just masculinity in general that makes you nervous?"

"I wish you wouldn't ask these questions now," she said sadly. "Please can't we have this discussion—"

"When?"

"In a few weeks. If you still want to," she said. He heard the unhappiness in her tone, but he was miles from being able to make any guess at the reason. Unless she was working something out in therapy? Or there was some guy who'd come back into her life?

Whoever he was, if he'd made Tallia afraid of herself like this, he'd like to kill the son of a bitch.

Funny the way two women had entered his life at the same time, almost the same day, that both of them should want to avoid serious involvement with him, and that he himself, while being sure that something, someone, had changed him on a deep level, could not really be sure which one had made the real impact. And that neither of them seemed to want to help him find out.

Maybe he was the one who needed a shrink.

On Date Four, Brad took Natasha to the races, but if he'd hoped that she would be any less Natasha on a hot afternoon at the track than she was in a club, he was mistaken.

She could pick winners, though. "Patsy Pokabout, Ah like that name," she announced before the first race, and Patsy Pokabout duly pulled out of the huddle a few yards from the finish line and streamed past the post at eleven to two.

She got as much pleasure from her fifty-dollar win as some women got from a diamond watch. He frowned in perplexity, and something at the back of his mind tried to surface.

"You're a lot like your sister," he said at last.

Tallia sobered when she heard that. "Who, Bel?" she asked carefully, knowing that her spontaneity had come close to giving her away. Thank God he had associated it with Bel and not her Tallia incarnation.

"I haven't met your other sisters," he pointed out mildly.

After that, she was careful to control her excitement.

Date Four, she thought afterwards. One more date, and then he'll never see Natasha again. I'll never hear him say *kiss me* again, never feel that passion burning me up without him even touching me....

Even if he did like Tallia, would he ever forgive her deceit when he found out?

She had one more date. It might be her last chance to experience Brad Slinger's passion before she risked killing it forever.

Oh, God, what should she do? What could she do?

10

He'd tried expensive elegance, back-to-nature, intimacy and aphrodisiacs, and excitement, Brad reflected. Time for a last-ditch attempt.

He was plotting his evening with Natasha, and this time he was determined that it would work. Tonight she was going to say "Kiss me, Brad." He would know how to take it from there. There would be no protest from her, he was pretty sure, once he had permission to...

He was getting hard just thinking about it, and that was no good. He had to think, not dream. He had to have a plan.

He hadn't planned a business takeover with the dedication he was now giving to the assault on Natasha Fox.

He knew he had an ally in his campaign—her own sexual interest in him. She'd denied it, but Brad had seen enough now to know for sure. He didn't know what her reasons were for resisting it, but he'd have put any money on her wanting him.

Dancing. That was the thing. It arrived suddenly, like most good inspirations. He had to get her on the dance floor, with first class music....

"May I hold you?" Brad asked, as the music changed from fast to slow, and Natasha automatically moved closer to him.

She couldn't have said no to save her life. She had no idea how much wine she had drunk, or how much buttery lobster she had eaten, but she was feeling light-headed and very, very sensuous. Especially staring into those determined blue eyes above her...half angry, half passionate, the expression in Brad Slinger's eyes was something she had to look away from to catch her breath.

She probably shouldn't have agreed to a date tonight. Neither of her had seen Brad for a whole week, and she was feeling far too desperate for his company. She certainly shouldn't have agreed to dance, but he'd asked her when a fast number was playing, and she hadn't thought of the danger she'd be in when fast changed to slow. Or hadn't wanted to think of it.

His voice as he spoke now, asking her permission to put his arms around her, was almost grim with suppressed feeling. It sent a shiver all over her body. She was almost certain that he had made up his mind to make love to her tonight, their last night together. She couldn't allow it, of course, she mustn't. But surely to dance a slow dance with him, in a crowded nightclub, would be safe enough?

She smiled and her head fell back on her neck as the music stroked her spine. Her head was light; she was not wearing the Natasha wig tonight. If Bel had been home she would never have gotten away with that, but Bel had gone to spend the weekend with the family, and Tallia was tired of not being herself with Brad. She had left off the blue contacts and the eyelashes, too. Only the bra remained.

"Can I be sure? I need to know," sang the singer,

haunting and slow. He must have asked them for the song, knowing it softened her. Why didn't he put his arms around her? Why didn't he touch her?

"Say it," he commanded, in a low, fierce voice. He was so close, his heat sending her crazy with longings that could never be fulfilled.

"Say what?"

"Say, touch me, Brad. Hold me."

"Touch me, Brad. Hold me," she whispered obediently.

She gasped aloud as his arms came around her, with more pent-up need than she would have believed existed in the universe. "Brad!" she cried softly.

"That's who I am, who are you?" he demanded in her ear, his voice sending feeling coursing down her bloodstream. She was barefoot, having kicked off the stilettos to dance. It meant her head tucked right into his neck, he noted in deep physical satisfaction.

"Do you want me to kiss you?" He raised a hand and touched a pulse in her throat. Feeling burned out from his fingertips all through her body. "I could kiss you here. Shall I do that?"

"Can I be sure?"

"Oh, Brad!"

He heard the Yes in her tone, and breathed slow and long in satisfaction. He had her now. She could pretend all night, if she wanted, but he had heard that unmistakable tone in her voice and knew he had won.

But it was not enough. He wanted to hear her say it. God knew he'd waited long enough. "Shall I?"

"Brad!"

"Say it!" he grated. His body was already hard against hers, and he knew she knew it. She knew what she was asking if she said it now. She couldn't cry wolf later.

Tallia felt drunk with the wildest desire she'd ever experienced. Desperately she tried to calculate her danger, play off what she wanted now against what that meant for later. She wanted him to kiss her, just once, wanted to feel that firm, angry mouth against her throat, her hair, her lips...but if he started, how would it end? If she could not resist now, in public, how would she resist later, if they were alone?

"Does love last forever?

"I need to know."

When they were alone, she amended. Because if she asked Brad to kiss her now, she knew without question that they would be alone later.

She couldn't think, couldn't calculate the danger, only her desire. She wanted him. For weeks now she had been resisting the deepest physical attraction she had ever felt for a man, and it hurt. It was hard and uncomfortable to resist, and delicious to submit...his touch was all she had dreamed it would be, sending chills of delight through skin and muscle and bone.

His mouth was so close to hers, his eyes staring into hers as though he was torn between passion and fury. She was alternately melting and freezing.

"What do you want, Brad?" she whispered, almost helpless.

"I want to pick you up and carry you to that table and make love to you on it," he told her grimly, watching her with hard, fierce eyes. "But I won't do that. That far I can control myself. I promise nothing else."

Passion leapt in her throat.

"We are going to make love tonight, Natasha," he said. "In the car, or on the beach, or my place, or yours...face it now, because I don't want any regrets later. I want you, and you want me, and this is the night. Now, tell me to kiss you, tell me to put my lips on your skin.''

"Does love last forever?"

Maybe it was that haunting question, repeated over and over by the singer. Maybe it was the yearning that the song created in her. Whatever happened afterwards, she could not say no to the powerful feeling coursing through her now. But what might happen afterwards...

"Does love last forever?" she asked him in a whisper.

"There is no forever," he said. "But it will last the night."

She looked into his eyes. Somewhere in the distance they were playing another song now. His body was an inch from hers, the heat leaping between them. She knew that his body was already prepared for her, as hers was for his. She was melted at the core.

She lifted her head and looked straight into his eyes, half fearful, half confident. "Kiss me, Brad," she cried in soft erotic command, and before she had finished speaking his mouth was pressed to hers, wild, hungry, drunk with passion.

His arms went around her back, hers around his neck, pulling each other closer as their mouths drank and drank and drank at the forbidden stream.

He was never really sure how he got them out of the nightclub after that kiss. All he knew was that once it started he nearly ate her alive. He realized dimly that he'd been wrong when he thought Natasha didn't get to him on a deep level. What drew him wasn't her gut intelligence or her physical beauty but her essence. He was like a bee in a flower——the colour had drawn him in, the perfume had trapped him, but what he really *wanted* was her pollen.

And he could get only so much of that in a public place without being arrested. He dragged his lips from hers, his arms from around her, and stood heaving for breath. The music had stopped, and people were applauding gently, so he must have been kissing her for the length of a whole song, but if so, it had only gone on long enough to prove that it wasn't long enough.

Tallia seemed to have gone blind and deaf. She blinked at him, and all she saw was those blue eyes staring at her through a mist. Her blood had been magnetized and now she was drawn to him uncontrollably. She had never felt physical excitement like this. Never felt such a deep, yearning need for someone else's body and soul and everything they were.

She knew he had to step away from her. There were people around them, they were in a public place. That tiny fingerhold was the only grip she had on ordinary reality. The rest was trying to hear against a storm.

"Let's get out of here," he said hoarsely.

His hand was on her wrist, he wasn't letting her go now that she had asked him to touch her, and he turned and led her back to the table to pick up their belongings and toss some money down. A waiter smiled and thanked him, but it didn't count as generosity, more as greed: he had no idea what the bill was, but he wanted to get Natasha alone.

The night was wet, making her skin glow under the streetlamps. She glowed anyway, her skin was luminous, and he'd lied to himself about everything, about what attracted him, what didn't. She drew him, and he didn't give a damn what she was, or where she went. If she went to Hollywood he would follow her, if she wanted a lab in the wilds of some jungle he would take her there and set it up for...no, no, his logical brain corrected him, that's a different woman, but he was beyond logic. All he knew was, he had found what he wanted in a woman and he had to take it.

"Your place?" he asked, because a woman felt safer on her own ground and he wanted her to feel safe. Then he remembered her sister, but Natasha had already said yes, so he drove there. Maybe she'd already arranged for Bel to be away tonight. In the elevator he punched the button for her floor, then turned and pulled her against him and lifted her chin with one hand and stared down into those blue eyes.

When he pushed the little button marked Three, Tallia barely noticed. Three? Was that where she lived? The elevator was quick; the doors were opening and he was starting down the hall when reality suddenly surfaced, and she gasped with audible shock. She would have forgotten. She had been going to take him to her own, Tallia's apartment—if he had not pushed the button. That little action brought her to herself. The danger she had been in sobered her as nothing else could have done.

She stopped in her tracks, bringing him to a standstill beside her. Her accent, reality, everything came back to her. How long had she been forgetting her accent, her role? She couldn't remember.

"What is it?" He turned and half-smiled at her, and the passion in his eyes was enough to make her drunk again. As if he suspected that she was suddenly nervous, he pulled her to him with one arm and kissed her again, and, half-carrying her, led her to the door of Bel's apartment.

She supposed she had known the end from the beginning tonight. She wanted Brad, and as Natasha she could have him. If she took her chance now. The future might lead anywhere.

She unlocked the door and they stepped inside. He only waited till she had locked the door again before sweeping her into his arms. He was afraid to give her time in case that momentary doubt in the hall returned.

"Where's the bedroom?" he growled, his voice sending anticipatory shivers up her spine, and Tallia felt the world reel as he swung her up off her feet. Her choice was made now. There was no going back.

One shoe had fallen off when he swung her up in his arms, the other as he laid her on the bed in the darkness. He bent over her and kissed her on the mouth. A light in the hallway cast its faint rays towards the bed, but she was in his shadow, and all was darkness.

But she did not need sight. She knew it was him with every cell, every pore. No one else had the power to stir her like this. She opened her mouth under his, inviting his deep kiss, while her arms wrapped his neck and enclosed his head. He was delicious. Taste and smell delighted in him. She opened her mouth wider. Her arms moved, and her hands found the muscles of his back and shoulders, strong and hard, and so right, as if he had been made just for her.

He lifted his head and his eyes glittered down at her in the reflected light, like those of a wild animal just beyond the reach of the fire...watching her, taking his time. Then their light was lost again as he bent his head, and she felt his lips against her throat, her neck, her breast. His hands found the slender straps of her dress and she felt his thumb slide one down over her shoulder and he kissed where it had been. She shivered, moaned, arched up into his kiss.

His hand slipped under her body as she did so, and moved against the zipper of her dress. His mouth pressed between her breasts as he drew the zip down the length of her spine, releasing the fabric. He stood and drew it from her body, and she lay with the faint light sculpting her perfect body.

He stood looking down at the long, silky legs, the curving hips covered by a brief strip of lace, the hips, stomach, breasts, shoulders, neck, mouth, eyes. Her beauty tore at him, as if its very existence put her out of his reach.

He pulled his shirt and pants off, then lay beside her on the bed, on the other side so that his own shadow did not hide her from his view, and began to caress her. Her skin was smooth and creamy to the touch, and his mouth followed his hand. He struggled for a moment with her bra, and she put a hand up to his and seemed to surface from a trance of pleasure.

"It's not all me, Brad," she whispered, but he did not understand what she was saying. The bra parted under his urgent fingers, and he lifted it from her and dropped it somewhere, his eyes on her full, creamy breasts.

His loins were so hard with wanting it was pain. But he wanted to take his time with her. He lifted her hand and pressed it against him, and saw her eyelids flutter.

Tallia was floating in and out of consciousness as pleasure and desire washed over her in waves. His hands kissed her and his mouth pressed her and she knew nothing but sensation. When he pressed her hand against him she moaned her understanding of the promise in his hard body, but that was all she knew.

His mouth suckled her breasts, trailed sensation across her body, made her cry out in anticipation and satisfaction. His hands pressed her and held her and told her she was his.

After a long, drunken time of reeling electric sensation, he moved over her, and she opened her mouth in needy expectation, waiting for the thrust that would make sense and perfection of all that had gone before. He was strong, virile, so much a man, and she opened her eyes and looked into his face as he waited one more second. The light outlined his strong jaw, his firm lips, was lost in the darkness of his eyes.

"Tell me what you want," he growled.

"You," she whispered. "I want you."

He groaned as his control snapped, and the thrust came at last, so strong and urgent that she cried aloud, wordlessly, her surprise and completion. Over and over, he pushed into her, pushed pleasure into her and took pleasure from her in the miracle of love.

When she felt crammed full of pleasure, and knew that any more would explode in her, she cried out. "No more," she pleaded, "no more!" Because something must give, but in her semi-conscious state she could not understand what, or how.

Brad's hand slipped under her hips then, and he drew her ferociously up to meet his body as he pounded into her, and then she knew that what would give was the floodgates that held back the torrent of sensation. They burst as delicious, flooding joy swept through her, and him, so that they were one being fused by the heat and light of pleasure. She cried his name as his body leapt in her, taking them both away on the flood.

11

Tallia awoke from a sweet dream, stretched and smiled a luxurious smile. So this was happiness. This was what she had been looking for, what her parents had, that had made it possible for them to stick together through life's hardest moments.

This was love. The thing that had caused those physical cravings, that fed her passion...she loved him, maybe had right from the first moment of meeting, if she hadn't been too confused with disguises and nerves and preconceptions to notice. *When he said "kiss me" that first night,* she thought, *if instead of deciding he was a rich man who just wanted sex with a beautiful woman, what if I'd understood that maybe he was responding to something special between us?*

She loved Brad Slinger. She smiled at the marvel of it, the sheer amazing wonder of what love was, and how it changed you, changed everything that you thought and were.

The bed beside her was empty. She rolled over and buried her face into the pillow where he had slept, trying to find his scent. How the smell of him had excited her, making her primitive and exalted both at once, as if she were half animal, half angel, and he had touched both parts of her. She sighed and shivered with the memory of delight. "Brad?" she called.

His watch lay on the little table under the lamp. Nine o'clock, and the sun was pouring in the windows. The night's rain had cleared. She lazily picked the watch up and clasped it around her own wrist, thrilled because it was too big for her, glorying in the weight of it. Like a handcuff, and she was handcuffed now, she was his, only to be tied to Brad would make her freer than she had ever been. She could fly now.

"Brad?" she called again, looking towards the door. Love changed everything, made her see what she should have seen before. All she had to do was tell him. Just tell him and explain. He loved her. She had been almost sure of that last night, that he had wanted to say it…she had wanted to say it, too, but she had saved it, savoured it. She had waited, but now, even if he did not say it, she could wait no longer.

She jumped up, naked and glowing in the morning sun, proud and grateful to be beautiful for him. Feeling her body had never been more beautiful than it was now, that she had not been beautiful until he touched her.

"Brad?" The bathroom door was open, and she moved on towards the sitting room and the kitchen.

The apartment was empty, except for her. The chain was off the door. He had gone.

He had probably gone out for the morning paper and some Danish pastries for their breakfast. Tallia bustled around Bel's kitchen, making coffee and setting the table on the little balcony that made her apartment such a pleasure in the morning. She sat and poured her own coffee, and drank it reading yesterday's paper. The coffee in the pot grew cold, and still Brad had not arrived.

For the hundredth time, Tallia consulted his watch. Nine-forty.

A thought occurred to her, and she trawled the apartment looking for a note in all the likely places, but there weren't many such places, and there was no note. Surely if he had had a business appointment, or some other pressing reason to leave her on a Sunday morning, he would have left one?

She began to worry that he had had an accident. But the thought of having to explain who she was and the circumstances made her realize how unlikely such a co-incidence was, and she did not allow herself to phone the police. There was a far more likely possibility staring her in the face. She recited the circumstances to herself aloud. "Last night, after weeks of him asking, I made love with a man for the first time. He left early this morning without leaving any message, and hasn't come back." She could just imagine any cop's reaction to that one, and she cringed in embarrassment.

At ten o'clock, the phone rang. Tallia leapt to snatch it up like a brand from the burning. "Hello?" she cried hopefully into the receiver.

"Tallia?" said Brad's voice. She shivered with the peculiar shifting of her reality. Brad had this number as belonging to Tallia.

"Hi, Brad!" she said. "What's up?"

"Tallia, are you free today?"

She blinked in amazement. "Am I—well, yeah, I guess so," she said, her voice rising curiously. It was pretty well the first time he had called her at home. Brad always got in touch with her at work.

"Great. Can you meet me down at the gym in half an hour?"

"Yes, but, Brad, what—" But with a quick, "Good, see you there," he had put the phone down.

She stood with her hand on the receiver, staring at nothing. What could be wrong? Brad had never asked her to work a weekend before, though she sometimes spent weekends at the lab or the gym. But this train of thought was completely driven out of her head by the sudden realization that if he had tried to call Natasha he would have used Tallia's own phone number!

Tallia dashed upstairs to her own apartment and ran to the answering machine. The message light was flashing, and she danced up and down impatiently as it rewound. He must have called Natasha, and, finding her out, had decided to work instead!

"Hi! It's me!" Bel's voice informed her. "I'm not going to stay tonight after all, be back home this evening. Talk to you then."

That was the only message. Tallia blinked and gazed at the machine as, ruthlessly refusing to produce any other message, it reset itself. But she had no time to think about it. Half an hour didn't give her a lot of time.

She had to put on her Tallia disguise, even though she expected that she would find a way today to tell Brad the truth. She couldn't just walk in on him as herself without any warning. So she carefully slipped her teeth into place and put on her brown lenses. But the day was going to be hot, and she contented herself with tucking her hair up under a baseball cap. She wouldn't take it off till she'd told him. She wore bluejeans and a white T-shirt, and looking at the result in the mirror, knew that if she carried on dropping the bits of her disguises, it wouldn't be long before Brad put one and one together and got one, anyway.

At the gym, he came over to her as she came in the door, but instead of leading her to the stairs and the basement space where the Virtual Reality room was being constructed, he took her to the building's main elevators, and before she had time to ask coherently where they were going, they were on the roof, where a helicopter was sitting on the helipad. Brad took her arm and led her under the rotors and inside.

"Brad, where on earth are we—" Tallia began, but he climbed into the pilot's seat and started the motors up, and that put an end to all conversation.

The copter lifted high above the city and moved gracefully off to the west, where the sea sparkled in the sun. Soon they were over the waters of the strait and moving north. Tallia sat in mystified silence for fifteen minutes, and then the direction he was taking suddenly made sense.

She turned to him and shouted, "Are we going to—?" and then broke off. How could she ask *Are we going to your cottage?* when as Tallia she didn't know of the cottage's existence?

But that was where they were going. She grew more certain of their destination with every minute that passed. What she could not fathom was the reason for it. It must be business that took them there, but in what possible way? If it was a pleasure outing, why hadn't he taken Natasha?

Nothing made sense.

Soon they were hovering, and she recognized the lake and the cottage as Brad began the descent. Then the horrible noise of the engine and rotors stopped, and her ears rang with the silence.

"Brad," she said, "what the heck is going on?"

He grinned sexily at her, and her heart turned over.

"We've both been working hard lately," he said. "Time we had a break."

He turned to drag a few shopping bags from the interior of the copter, then clambered out. Tallia sat there utterly stupefied until he came around to open her door for her. "Come on!" he commanded with a grin. "The water's fine!"

"I don't have a suit," she protested, following him to the cottage. Inside the kitchen, he set down several supermarket bags stuffed with packages and leafy green vegetables, then handed her a smart plastic bag from one of Vancouver's most expensive women's shops.

"There are a few in different sizes in there. One should fit you," Brad said casually, and, pulling open the fridge, began to unload his purchases onto its mostly empty shelves.

Tallia felt as if she were standing in the whirlwind. "Brad, I thought you were calling me about business!" was all she seemed capable of saying.

"On a Sunday?" He lifted out a brown-paper-wrapped package that was oozing blood and she knew that it contained steaks for the barbecue. He looked at her. "I never do business on a Sunday. People who don't save one day for relaxation get heart attacks. Also, they make money at the expense of everything else in life, and Tallia, money isn't that important."

"Yes, but—"

He turned her around and pointed. "Go into that room and get changed." He gave her a little push in the right direction and patted her butt for good measure. Tallia blinked at him over her shoulder. His attitude to her had changed. He had always been so careful with her. But now he seemed—Tallia could hardly believe it—he seemed determined, almost *predatory*.

As if it was Tallia's turn to be on the receiving end of Brad Slinger's seductive charm.

All the bathing suits in the bag were bikinis. Tallia put on the one that gave the most coverage, which wasn't saying much. It was a tropical patterned Lycra, a pretty blue-green with splashes of deep pink, snug-fitting, with high-cut legs and a halter top. She tied her hair up into a tight knot on top of her head, and hoped that Brad wouldn't notice the colour change until she'd found her moment to explain.

"Ah, you've dyed your hair!" he said approvingly, when she appeared outside. "It looks very sexy, Tallia."

"Thank you," was all she could say. He was already stripped down to his own swim trunks, and Tallia caught her breath and stood looking at him in wonder. He did not realize it, but she knew his body now, and the sight of his bare chest and arms, his strong thighs, made her shiver with the memory of pleasure. Suddenly the night just past flooded over her, and with a smile that she could not repress tugging at the corners of her lips, and a slight pinkening of her cheeks, she dropped her head.

"Right, this is going well," said Brad, putting down the lid on the barbecue. "Ready for a swim?"

He caught her hand and they ran together to the water's edge and splashed in. They fell forward and simultaneously began a steady crawl towards the middle of the lake. They swam side by side; she was sure that Brad was pacing himself to her. After a few minutes of steady exercise, he pulled up to tread water. Tallia did the same, and for the first time she noticed that there was a tiny little island just in front of them in the middle of the lake.

"Oh! I never noticed that la—" She choked and

coughed. She had nearly said *last time*. "From the beach," she amended.

"There's a kind of optical illusion until you know what you're looking for," Brad agreed. "Shall we do a circuit?"

By the time they had swum a couple of circuits she was ready for a rest, and they stumbled up the steep sides of the little island and subsided onto the warm rocks. Neither could resist the temptation to lie back and let the sun bake them. They lay side by side—much as they had lain last night, she thought—panting from their exertions.

"That was fabulous!" she said, when she had breath. "It's such a pleasure to swim in fresh water for a change! You're so lucky to own your own private lake!"

Then she bit her tongue. As Tallia she did not know that he owned this lake. Brad didn't seem to notice the mistake, but it was time to put an end to her charade. Tallia sat up, drawing her knees up, and rested her arms on her knees. All around her were the noises of nature that we call stillness—the gulls overhead, the birds in the trees, the hum of insects, the intermittent rustle of small wild animals.

"Brad," she began, "about Natasha Fox, I—"

Brad sat up, smiling at her in a way that melted her bones, and lifted one hand to stroke back a strand of hair from her forehead.

"Tallia," he said softly, "don't worry about Natasha Fox. She means absolutely nothing to me, and I am not seeing her anymore."

Tallia blinked, stared, and blinked again. "Wh-what?"

"Natasha Fox is the kind of woman that gets into a man's blood briefly. Then, one day, the madness has passed, and if he's got any sense, a man is grateful it has.''

''And it passed?'' she choked, wondering how she could get the words out. ''How?''

She wondered if he would admit to her that it had ''passed'' because he had finally got Natasha where he wanted her—in bed. Somewhere inside her a distant anger was starting to burn.

''The how isn't important,'' he told her, with a kind of paternalistic authority that she had never seen in him before. He smiled as if he knew why she was having doubts, and they were all very female and foolish. She had never seen him like this. Distantly she wondered whether he adjusted his personality to the woman he was with, but brushed the thought aside.

''Does she know it's over?''

He nodded. ''Our agreement was for five dates. We had our last date last night.''

''I see. And now it's my turn, is that it? How many dates do you want with me?'' Tallia asked dryly.

He smiled quizzically at her. ''You sound annoyed, Tallia. What's the matter?''

''It's not very pleasant to discover I'm on a list and the woman who preceded me on it has been written off, so it's my turn.'' Tallia could hardly speak over the feeling that choked her throat. She got to her feet abruptly and flung herself into the water, where she started to swim for shore.

Her head was a whirlwind of conflicting thoughts. It had meant nothing to him, then! While she had been falling in love, Brad had merely been getting Natasha *out of his system!* God, what could she do now? It was clear he intended to move straight on and get Tallia out of his system, too, and what defences did she have? Just being on the same rock with him made her sexually dizzy!

She needed time to think, but time was clearly just what Brad did not intend to allow her to have. He followed her into the water after giving her a head start, and was soon swimming beside her with long, sure strokes. She felt like something being guarded by a dog, and realized for the first time that what had seemed to her to be Brad understanding Tallia's "fear" of men had been nothing more than a man prepared to hold back his attack on her defences until he'd got another woman off his plate.

By the time she had reached shore she still hadn't made up her mind what to do. She could hardly get all self-righteous with him over his dumping of another woman without revealing that she knew much more about the subject than he knew she knew, and in any case, self-righteousness was not exactly appropriate as a prelude to telling him that she had been duping him for weeks.

In fact, it now seemed impossible to confess the truth. He had already said it was out of sight out of mind with Natasha. Except, perhaps, for a feeling of annoyance at being had, the fact that two women were one wouldn't make any impact on him, would it? Tallia took stock. She was in love with Brad, but if she had mistaken his feelings for Natasha, she had no hope that his feelings for Tallia were any stronger. She was certain they were not. So Tallia, if she was so foolish as to give in to what she knew was coming, would have nothing but a double measure of heartbreak.

If she could just get through the day, she might be able to think. She felt so stupid right now, her brain not functioning except to pour feelings through her system, making her heart beat in her ears. She stumbled up onto the shore, with Brad right beside her. Before she had any idea of his intentions, his arms were around her from behind, and he was pulling her body against his. He bent and pressed his mouth against her neck.

"You're so beautiful, Tallia," he whispered, as shivers ran up and down her body under the caress of his lips over two square inches of skin. She wanted to pull away, but the memory of last night kindled in her brain, making her weak with sheer physical need, as if after one night she were already addicted to his lovemaking.

"Brad," she protested feebly, but in reply his mouth only travelled further. Down her neck, towards her shoulder, pausing as his finger pulled the halter strap of her top to let his mouth, with the utmost sexiness, find the skin underneath.

"Let yourself go, and enjoy the day, Tallia," he said. Against her buttocks she could feel his flesh beginning to stir, and he let her go. Tallia gulped in air to steady herself, and knew that if he hadn't done so, she could not have gotten away from him. She must be careful not to let him get so close a second time.

Why not? whispered a treacherous voice inside her. *He's a dream lover, and he wants to love you.*

At the thought of not resisting, her knees gave way, and she sank down onto the canvas lounger and tried to figure out what kind of mess she was letting herself in for. Brad wanted to make love to Tallia because she was a new conquest, but she knew that she was not. He had already made love to her as Natasha. If she told him *now* who she was, he wouldn't want her anymore, would he? It was the one way to save herself from any more heartache.

On the other hand, the only way to get more of Brad

was to continue to lie to him, and she was already hooked. If she had to learn to get along without him, why sooner rather than later? Why not put off the moment for as long as possible, by letting him continue to believe that Tallia was a new conquest?

What should she do?

12

———◄———

Brad had wrapped two potatoes in foil and was now stuffing them into the hot coals of the barbecue. "These'll take about an hour," he said. "Now, will you have something to drink?"

Without waiting for an answer he turned and moved into the cottage, returning with a bottle of champagne and two glasses. With practised ease, he popped the cork and filled the glasses without letting the foam slip over the brim. He handed her one and then picked up the other to clink with hers.

"To mutual satisfaction!" he said, his eyes fixing hers seductively.

He was acting like a Casanova! She disliked it, but she also could not resist Brad's sheer physicality. He was the most attractive man she had ever met, there was something about him that excited her without him raising a finger; and now, in addition, she knew that he was also an expert, delicious lover, a man designed as if for her, who had sought out her tender spots, discovered her sexual yearnings, as one born to the task. But he was also, it was clear, a man without any sexual scruples, or maybe even discrimination. When she thought of how he had said that his friend Jake went through women more frequently than cars, she wanted to scream. Brad himself, it appeared, went through women at a rate of five hot dinners to one!

But if last night had showed her his usual modus operandi, there was no doubt he deserved his success rate, whispered the little voice of desire in her head.

She finished the champagne in her glass far too quickly. She had been thirsty and should have drunk a glass of water first, but before she could get up to get some, he had refilled her glass, and it seemed like too much trouble. They sat in the sun, feet up, as she drank the second glass and got sleepier and sleepier, and if his eyes watched her too closely, she was feeling too good to protest.

"Let me show you how to put that bed flat and then I'll put some sun tan oil on you so you can relax while I cook," Brad said after she had drained her second glass of deliciously cool, heady champagne.

Tallia smiled drowsily. "Oh!" was all she said. The tone of his voice suggested that he did not intend to cook while she was relaxing, or at least, not until he had made sure, in his own way, that she was completely relaxed, but she was not capable of resisting, certainly not now that she had virtually gulped so much champagne. She suddenly reminded herself that she had had only coffee for breakfast, waiting for Brad to come back with some pastries. Two glasses of champagne on an empty stomach, a beautiful day with the sun smiling warmly down, a breeze...*a loaf of bread, a jug of wine, and thou,* in other words...these were not the tools with which women usually resisted the advances of handsome, sexy, half-naked men with marvellous hands and eyes, she told herself as, under Brad's command, she lay on her stomach on the flat canvas bed and gave herself up to whatever he had in store for her.

She heard the crack of the lid, and then the scent of coconut and banana wafted over her senses. She felt him unhook her bikini straps, leaving her sun-warmed back completely bare for him, and then his hands, slippery with the sweet-smelling oil, were unexpectedly firm against her skin.

His fingers found the tensed muscles and tension points in her neck, and worked them, unknotting all the stiffness that hours in front of her computer had produced, making her feel loose and relaxed. He took his time with every inch, but still he had moved on to her shoulders before it had sunk in that Brad was not merely protecting her skin from the sun. He was giving her a massage. She sighed with unconsciously expressed pleasure.

His fingers moved all along her spine, kneading and working each vertebra and its attendant muscles, working from a base where her bikini bottom started, up and up to her neck, time after time. As his strong thumbs kneaded the base of her spine, his fingers clasped her hips for traction, and she was reminded of the way he had held her last night, pulling her hips into him as he thrust over and over into her body, and she felt faint with desire for him.

Sometimes he stroked, sometimes he kneaded, sometimes he soothed, sometimes he worked the muscle deeply, but always, always, he sent messages of delight to her nerves and senses. The smell of the coconut oil, the heat of the sun and his hands, the strength in his fingers that he could reduce to tender caressing at a stroke, and his own nearness...Tallia lost all resistance.

His hands worked her arms, her elbows, wrists and hands, sliding his fingers in between hers in a gesture more deeply erotic than she would ever have dreamed, forcing her fingers wide apart to take the greater width of his. Now and then she moaned her appreciation, but he didn't seem to need any response, and finally she gave herself up to the pure luxury of accepting pleasure without the responsibility of gratitude.

With soft seduction, his hands moved up her back, and then to her underarms, along the exposed sides of her sensitive breasts and down the sides of her body to her hips again. Each stroke was magic and excitement. She was melting inside, her body was preparing for him long before he even reached her legs in his exploration.

He began at her feet, taking one in a firm grip with one hand while the thumb of the other pressed into the sensitive sole, sending shivers up her body to her centre and then out to all of her. He pulled and stroked her toes, and her hair lifted on her head as his touch shivered through her body, cell by cell. He used his firm strength on heel and ankle, and then moved up to her calf, building the delicious mental and physical anticipation in her, heading for the spot that was waiting for his touch, taking his time.

Then at last he massaged her thigh, his hands slipping on her oily skin as he moved in wider and wider circles, climbing from knee to her lower body. His hands slipped, and pressed briefly against the centre of her body through her bikini bottoms, igniting her so that she almost moaned with excitement. It happened again and again as he worked her upper thigh, exciting her but leaving her unfulfilled, so that she wished he would press his hand there...he moved up to her buttocks, and slipped his fingers under the edges of her bikini leg, all unconsciously, as if he were hardly aware that his hands were so close to her sex, or making her melt with the promise of release....

Back to the other foot, and the same long, slow strokes. This time her anticipation was even greater, for knowing what would come when he reached her thigh...and again, his strong hands slipped in the oil on her upper thigh and he brushed her again and again in tantalizing contact...his fingers moved all around the edge of the bikini leg till she couldn't have spelled her own name. Then he put one hand on each thigh, and his thumbs and fingers moved together along her inner thighs, out and over her buttocks along the line of the high-cut leg, under, around, and back again to between her legs, his thumbs always going just under the edge of the fabric and no further.

"Turn over," he commanded softly, when she was wild with this tantalization of her senses.

She could hardly have spoken, except to beg him for what she wanted. She raised herself, and her breasts lifted free of the halter top. With a feeble pretence at decorum she put her hand under it to clasp it to her breasts as she rolled over, and left it resting on her chest as she arrived on her back.

He started with her face, with the gentlest stroking motion across her forehead, around her eyes, her cheeks, and then, more firmly, his thumb rubbed oil into her lips. Even her ears received his attention, making her nerves sing yet another harmony as he pressed the creases and gently pulled her lobes between his thumbs and fingers.

Once she opened her eyes, but his were on his task, and she closed them again. He moved down to her neck, pressing the sensitive area behind her ears, making the lightest strokes over her throat. When he arrived at her chest and shoulders, he lifted the halter top of her bikini without a word and tossed it aside, and her breasts shivered in anticipation.

He stroked the full creaminess of her breasts with gentle firmness, and fitted his hands below her breasts, stroking upward in a curve and around again and down over her breasts, till they ached with the strength of her desire. Then she was electrified by sensation that rippled through her, and simultaneously she felt a wet warmth...gasping, she opened her eyes again, and saw that he had taken her nipple into his mouth. The shot of sensation was like electricity zinging to every nerve and cell in her body. She breathed and arched her head back, while Brad released one urgent bud of her flesh and moved to take the other between his lips. His lips pressed it and his tongue stroked it, and by the time he was done with that, Tallia was stifling moans.

Down her stomach the stroking continued, across her abdomen in endless curling strokes, and then again he retreated to her feet and worked his slow, deliberate way up past ankles, calves, knees, and thighs.

She was helplessly melted now, too far gone either to resist what he was doing, or beg him to continue. She could only experience what he chose to give her as he firmly spread her legs to give him better access to her upper thighs, and the motion and the pressure of his hands as he did so made her gasp in the deepest sexual anticipation she could ever remember experiencing.

His thumb rested deliberately on her mound, then, and through the thin Lycra he stroked the centre to which every nerve and every yearning cell was now attached.

She was lightheaded with the sensations he was creating in her. She felt faint. She no longer saw the sun against her eyelids but bursts of blackness as her tension built and built.

He pushed her thighs apart again, and now his fingers pulled aside the fabric that kept her from him, and she felt the breeze brush that part of her and knew she was naked to him. His thumb found the soft, slippery spot that was waiting for his touch, and now nothing impeded the sensations that streamed through her from head to toe, and her body leapt as the tension built higher and higher, desire and delight like two perfectly matched horses taking her to her destination.

She cried out as she arrived and the honey of pleasure flowed through her under his touch. His thumb stroked and caressed until her trembling subsided, and then his hands released her. She smiled, feeling the hot sweetness flow through her muscles. "Thank you—" she began, but stopped when she felt his hands at the edge of her bikini, felt him pull it down over her hips and down her legs, and then she really was naked, and he was ruthlessly pushing her thighs even further apart, and the next thing she felt was the heat and wet of his mouth, and her own body's sharp reaction as her pleasure climbed to another level.

His tongue was merciless. It stroked with tiny, rasping vibrations that drove her crazy with a burning sensation that she had never experienced in her life before. This time the pleasure built from and in a part of her that was all new, the sweetest vats of honey, that had been lying deep inside her without her ever being aware of it. She thought she would explode and die before release came, because he did not speed his tormenting pace, or increase the pressure in the way that would have ensured her immediate sweet release. Instead he simply went on and on with the tenderest, gentlest motion, and everything in her seemed to stop, as if she were listening with all her being for a distant sound. At last she heard it, felt these sensations building to a peak, and the cries that came to her throat now were very new. Not moans, but small panting sighs of surprise and wonder as throughout her body a thousand little sacs simultaneously exploded and released hot honey that ran, liquid and sweet, along a thousand new tracks of pleasure all at once. Only when the peak of this unbelievable sensation had passed did moans arise in her throat, telling him of her gratitude.

Her mind floated away on the wings of pleasure to a place of perfect peace.

She was not sure how long she had been in that place, or whether she had slept. She came to to find herself in the shade of a large beach umbrella, and the delicious smell of steaks grilling on the air. She sat up lazily to find that Brad had draped a large shirt over her, and she gratefully slipped her arms into it and pulled it around her body.

"Hello," he said. "Nice nap?"

She felt shy with him. She had been the greedy recipient of the pleasure he gave her, but she had given him none. She felt as if someone had seen her naked while remaining clothed himself. She had revealed a part of herself no one had ever seen, or at least not since she had drunk from her mother's breast, with total and oblivious dedication to her own needs and pleasures.

"How long did I sleep?"

"Lunch is nearly ready," Brad responded, as if that were the answer to her question. "If you want to take a quick swim to cool off, now's your chance."

The lake was deliciously tempting in the afternoon sun, looking fresh and clear and cool. She saw that the bikini she had been wearing was neatly draped over the end of the lounger, but as if Brad had opened some new pathway of freedom in her, she found that she wanted to go into the water naked. She stood up, her crossed arms holding the loose shirt closed over her breasts, and stepped down to the wooden pier. She dropped the shirt from her body and then slipped over the side into deep water.

It was heaven. She had never felt so at one with the universe in all her life. She was the water and the fish in the water, and the sunshine glinting on its surface, the sky, the breeze…with lazy abandon she struck out towards the little island, feeling the cool embrace of the lake over her skin with total and complete pleasure.

It wasn't just the pleasure he had given her body, of course. It was the joy that loving him made in her soul. Probably she should worry about that, about where it would lead her. But not yet, she told herself, as her wet arm flashed in the sunlight and clove the water with a perfection that was all new. Not yet. She would worry later.

She pulled on her bikini and the shirt when she had dried herself off, and sat down at the table while Brad served the meal of luscious salad, charcoal-grilled garlic steak and charcoal-baked potatoes and sour cream.

"I'd sure gain weight if I hung around with you very long," she observed, slicing through meat as tender as butter and popping a delicious bit into her mouth.

He raised his eyebrows for explanation. "Well, you just make food too delicious to resist."

"You're far too slim to think that a few meals would make you fat."

She opened her mouth to tell him that she was already a lot bigger than the new breed of model, that the demand now was for young girls who looked starved, closed it again, and started over. "I will have to do a lot of extra exercise this week to work off the last two meals I've had with—''

She broke off again. Every subject seemed a danger area today. Brad was looking at her, his eyebrows enquiringly up. Tallia smiled and shrugged.

"Diets are boring," she said in as casual a manner as she could summon. "Where did you learn to cook like this?"

"What were you going to say?" he pursued lightly. "The last two meals you've had with—"

Tallia couldn't think of any syntactical magic that would turn that statement into something innocuous. It was a social hand grenade just waiting to go off. Last night's lobster and garlic butter had been eaten by *Natasha,* a fact she had reminded herself of just in time.

At last she said, "Last night I had dinner with someone who was also trying to—" She broke off.

"Seduce you with food?" he supplied.

She smiled and shrugged. It wasn't a lie, not literally, but still she hated telling it.

Brad put a piece of dripping steak into his mouth and chewed for a moment with obvious sensual pleasure, watching her. "Did he succeed?"

Tallia blushed bright red. "What a question! None of your business!" She realized that sounded like a yes, which was both true and false. But there was no way out of the corner she'd crawled into. Anyway, maybe she didn't want to. If Brad wasn't seriously interested in her, she would rather he did not know the state of her heart. When this was over she would go away and lick her wounds in private.

Brad smiled without any sign of jealousy. "Well, you're a very sexy lady, and I'm sure there's plenty for both of us."

"Well, for as long as you're likely to need it, anyway," she riposted.

"Now, what makes you think I have short-term designs, Tallia?"

"A cavalier attitude towards the last name on your list gave me a clue."

"But you might be the one to capture and hold my heart forever," he teased. She knew it meant nothing. He was not seriously trying to seduce her with the hope of a meaningful affair, and yet her heart beat hard at his words. The one thing she must not do was to start imagining that Brad would ever get serious with her. Until this morning she had believed he might be in love with Natasha, but she must never let herself hope again.

And maybe it wasn't his fault that he had a kind of intensity that made a woman feel like the only thing in his life.

She smiled sweetly at him. "But, Brad, you might not be the one to capture mine," she pointed out.

Then she wished she hadn't tried to outplay him, because his eyes got darker suddenly, just as if the sun had gone behind a cloud, and he was looking at her with the same look that Natasha had seen in his eyes last night.

13

"So," said Jake, standing up from the patio fridge with two cans of beer in his hand. He tossed one to Brad. They were sitting by Jake's pool, their feet up, and had, as usual, turned the sound down on the halftime show. "So how are you getting along with—ah, the inventor and beauty queen?"

Brad held the beer to one side and snapped the lid, then quickly put his mouth over the opening to contain the foam. "I just dropped Tallia off before coming here, as it happens."

"Tallia—plain but bright, right?"

"In your opinion," Brad agreed placidly.

"You spent the day with her?"

Brad nodded, then reached out and picked up a handful of tortilla chips.

"How did it go?"

"About as planned."

"So why are we male bonding now?"

"Jake, you know we had a date to watch the game. I've got five bucks riding on the Lions."

"They aren't going to win just because you're watching the game."

Brad dug in to the guacamole and tossed the chip into his mouth. "You never know."

"You spent the day with her and then dropped her home at six o'clock to come and watch a football game that promises to be a walkover with your good buddy." Jake repeated the information as if it were in a foreign language.

"Jake, that's your problem, you're too greedy. Learn finesse. Always leave 'em wanting more," Brad said expansively.

"My motto is, if you leave them wanting more, they tend to get it from someone else."

"Not Tallia."

"And Natasha, is she still a going concern?"

Brad took a long drink. "She wasn't going to be, I admit, but somehow I find myself intrigued to discover whether she would see me again."

"You wouldn't want me to take her off your hands, run a little interference for you?"

Brad lowered his beer and gazed at his friend. "Jake, you know that I know that you know that both these women are essential to my happiness and that I'd chop your arm off if you so much as tried to shake the hand of either of them."

"And you have the nerve to call me greedy?"

"There's a difference between greed and necessity."

"You're getting into deep water, my friend," Jake warned, with some relish, as if he would like to see Brad in over his head with a woman. Or women. "Do they, ah—how shall I put it—know about each other?"

Brad lifted his mouth from his beer and grinned. "Naturally. They live in the same building."

Jake's head went up. "Of course. And how do they manage that?"

"Natasha rooms with her sister."

Jake shook his head, grinning.

"I've been told they have a nodding acquaintance in the elevator."

"Playing a dangerous game, boy. You should put a stop to it. Where is it all going to end?"

Brad reached for the remote and booted up the sound as the playing field came back onscreen. "Just where I want it to, Jake," he grinned, and then sobered. "I hope."

"Natasha?"

"Brad?"

"Yeah, it's me. How are you?"

"I'm—uh, Ah'm just fine, Brad. Why?" Tallia's heart was beating so hard she could hardly hear his next speech. After their meal this afternoon, Brad had mentioned a long-standing date to watch the football game with a friend, packed her into the helicopter and flown home without any hint of wanting anything more from her. "It's a tradition with us," he'd explained, and really, she had no right to complain, although she was wishing he wanted to spend the evening, and maybe the night, with her. She was still in a sexual daze.

"*'Why?'* You think it's unusual for me to want to know how you are after last night?"

"Oh! Well, no, but—"

"I'm sorry I ran out on you like that, but I got an emergency call very early and didn't want to wake you. I've been working all day."

"You have?" Tallia asked, fighting not to let her indignation show. For two cents she would tell him that she had just seen herself in the corridor and been told she'd just spent the day at Brad's cottage...but she decided, hastily, that it would be better to let him tell the lie.

"Yeah, I just got out of a strategy meeting." Well, he had discussed strategy of a kind with Jake. "I hope it's not too late to call. Are you busy?"

"No, I've been watching the game," she said.

"Really? You watch Canadian football? I've got five bucks on that game," he told her. "Did the Lions win?"

"Y'all have five bucks on the Lions?" Tallia asked softly.

"That's right."

"Ah'm afraid you all just lost five dollars, Brad. The Roughriders walked all over them."

Brad blinked. "Were you watching—" and cut himself off, because what he had been going to say was *Were you watching the same game I was?* He frowned into the receiver. The Lions had won it 28-17! They'd pretty well put it in the bag with five minutes on the clock, and an interception and a ninety-nine-yard runback for touchdown in the last minute and a half had put it beyond dispute. It had been the best game of the season so far. Why was she lying to him about watching the game? What the heck had she been doing with her time since— "Right to the end?" he said instead.

"Oh, yeah, Ah just now turned the set off." Tallia grinned nervously at Bel, who was making curious faces. She didn't know why she was telling him the fib. Maybe to teach him that two could play at his game. If he wasn't watching the game, what *had* he been doing since dropping Tallia off, with no mention of when they might see each other again?

She had only watched the game because he would be watching and it had seemed like a connection with him. Had he lied to Tallia, or was he lying now? And either way, why?

"Right. Well, I guess I just lost five bucks, then."

"Something tells me you'll survive, though."

"The blow to my pocket, yes. The blow to my pride is a different thing altogether," he said, and heard it ring with the kind of extra resonance that some speeches do have.

"Well, it was kind of y'all to ring, Brad."

"Natasha, when can I see you again?" he said hastily. Tallia gasped. *"See me?"*

"Why does that surprise you?"

"Because—because—" *Because you told Tallia you weren't going to see me anymore, that's why!* She wanted to cry. "Your five dates are over, Brad," she said firmly.

"Come on, Natasha, we can't leave it like this, can we?" Brad said, with seductive persuasiveness. "Have you eaten? Let's have dinner."

"Tonight?" she exclaimed, aghast. How could he *do* that? Make incomplete love to one woman and then leave her all up in the air and want a different woman three hours later?

"Ah'm dieting today. Ah won't be eating dinner."

"Let's have a drink, then."

"Alcohol has calories, Brad."

"Drink mineral water," he begged.

"Brad, we broke my rule last night, and correct me if Ah'm wrong, but y'all got what you wanted for your money, isn't that so?" Her voice betrayed a certain bitterness.

"That's putting a pretty unfriendly construction on things. Come on, Natasha."

She couldn't believe the way her heart was pounding. Although his lovemaking this afternoon had been incredible, she had still been left in a state of wanting more. It had been an hour of foreplay, and then no main course, and her body was still rushing with sensual rivers anytime she let herself think of Brad or the things he had done. She wanted to see him almost desperately, and if he had called Tallia she would have said yes like a shot. Well, with an attitude like his, no doubt if Natasha turned him down he'd call Tallia.

"Brad, I'm sor—"

In the middle of her refusal, she stopped. What if she said no and he *didn't* call Tallia? What if he called woman number three instead? What if he never called Tallia again? If he'd lied to Tallia about his feelings for Natasha, maybe he'd lied about his feelings for her, too! Maybe it was *Tallia,* not Natasha, whom he had got out of his system with one encounter. Going as Natasha might be her only way to see him again.

Experience his expert lovemaking again.

The thought of never making love to Brad again was like a cold hand on her heart.

"All right, Brad," she said sadly.

"I'll pick you up in half an hour."

Bel looked at her sister. "How long are you going to keep this up, Tal?"

"As long as he wants to see either of me," Tallia said simply. Fortunately she had washed her hair as soon as she came in this afternoon, and now it was only a matter of moussing and crimping and spraying it into a Natasha mane.

"He's a playboy. He's going to break both your hearts and then leave you cold."

"He has already broken my heart. And it won't make it any better if I stop seeing him. Someday I know I'll have to face living without Brad Slinger all the rest of my lives, but I'm going to put the evil moment off as long as possible.''

''Don't you have any pride?''

Tallia's eyes met her sister's in the mirror. ''That's what you don't understand yet, Bel, because you aren't in love. When you really love someone, pride is completely unimportant.''

The sisters looked at each other. ''Well, if that's the case, I hope I never fall in love!''

Tallia shook her head. ''No. You don't understand. It's not a thing you can wish not to happen to you, even if it turns out badly. Love is just—it's the secret of the universe. You can't wish not to learn the secret of the universe, Bel.''

Bel shivered. ''Why don't you just tell him, Tal?''

''Before, it was because I was afraid he'd pull my funding, and Damon's, too. Now I know he wouldn't care enough to bother. He's not seriously interested in either of me. But now I'm afraid if he felt I'd made him look like a fool, he'd stop seeing both of me. His pride wouldn't like it.''

''Tallia—''

She put up a hand. ''Bel, I told you. It won't hurt me less if I stop seeing him now. At least I'll have a few memories this way. I don't think anything could be worse than not having any memories.''

Bel trailed her back into the bedroom and watched as her sister dressed. ''Why are you wearing that bra? He already knows you're half stuffing.''

Tallia resolutely carried on with her dressing. ''Because he has seen my figure as Tallia now, and whatever he knows, this will make it more difficult for him to recognize me.''

''You think he won't recognize your body when

you're und—'' Bel broke off and shook her head in confusion. The whole thing was beyond her now. A complete mystery. She had never seen her sister like this.

Natasha, her makeup and costume complete, turned around. "Natasha only evah makes love in the dark, honeychile," she said, in her breathiest voice.

"He is bound to find out!"

"Sooner or later," Tal said, her eyes suddenly dark. "I am going to squeeze as much as I can in before that moment."

"You're looking very beautiful tonight."

They were sitting on the terrace of his penthouse apartment, looking out over the water and watching the sunset. It was a beautiful place, the entire top floor of a small building right on English Bay. The apartment was completely surrounded by the wide landscaped terrace, a garden in the sky. At one end there was even a greenhouse. It was the first time she had seen it, but it was a place, she had discovered, she instantly felt comfortable, at home.

Natasha smiled. "Beauty goes skin deep, Brad. Don't y'all ever wonder what else there is to me?"

"I do. Tell me about yourself. Where were you raised?"

Natasha kicked herself. The last thing she wanted was him asking her questions about her background. She shrugged and smiled. "Ah had a very ordinary upbringing."

"No poor-hillbilly-made-good stories?"

She laughed. "'Fraid not. Is that what you'd like to hear? Mah daddy is a high school teacher and mom gives piano lessons. What about—'' She paused for a moment, trying to remember which one of her he had told about his mother's abandonment of him. They'd gone on to talk about Hollywood, so it was a pretty safe guess it had been Natasha. "You? Were you raised here in Vancouver?"

He nodded. "Kits. With a small telescope I can see my old house from here."

"Does your father still live there with his new family?"

"No, he sold it and moved to a new place when he married. Where does your family live now?"

He was one irritating man. Most men were happy to talk about themselves. In her experience anything else was just preliminary to what they considered the main topic of interest in life.

"Oh, that reminds me! Ah have your watch! Y'all left it behind." She smiled at him as she dug in her evening bag and drew it out. Brad took it from her and laid it on the table beside him.

"When you all didn't come back, Ah thought maybe the watch was left deliberately, as a kind of memento," she confessed.

"Would you have liked to keep it?"

Natasha frowned. "Ah near as dammit flushed it down the toilet, Brad. But then common sense prevailed."

"Did Bel say that your family lives up in the va—?"

"Oh, look! Don't y'all just love it when the sun finally touches the water and that golden glow just sparkles out over the waves like that?"

Brad grinned. "I certainly do. How many sisters and brothers did you say you have?"

She paused a moment, drinking in the beauty while her brain raced. This was like the third degree, and her brain was just so slow tonight. She wished he would shut up and make love to her. Didn't he want to make love to her? If not, why was he sitting close enough to burn her skin? At last she remembered that Bel was Natasha's sister and therefore it was Natasha who had the four siblings.

"What?—oh, four. There's five of us," she said absently, turning briefly from the amazing beauty before her.

He was sitting even closer now. He had put her onto a lounger with her feet up, and he was beside her in a straight chair, his elbows on his knees, bending over her. Every time he shifted, she could feel the ripple of response on her skin, as if his aura brushed her. Her arms ached to go around him.

"What are their names?" he asked softly, bending closer.

"Ah—well, Bel you've met, and there's—uh—" She could hardly remember their real names, let alone whether she had given him false ones before. "Um, Russ—his name's really Cyrus, but he doesn't like it—and Dom and Jordan."

"—?"

She blinked into his blue, blue eyes, and realized she had gone deaf. "What did you say?" she breathed, as Brad, caught in the magnetic field at last, involuntarily leaned closer. His mouth seemed to hover by her cheek.

"I said—"

"Brad," she whispered, interrupting him.

"Natasha?"

"Kiss me, you fool," breathed Natasha.

He hadn't really expected something like this, though he had maybe been hoping for it, if only as a sign, he admitted to himself. Brad had planned to take his time, but he was no proof against this plea. The words had barely died on her lips before he smothered them with his own. He reached over her to put his glass down on the table on her other side, but his passion leapt so quickly to white heat that her own glass was forgotten and spilled its contents over her lap. Her spasmodic cry as the ice settled against her thighs made him break off. He took her glass and moved it out of danger. Then he slipped his arms under her and stood up, lifting her clear of the chaise before letting her feet slide to the ground as he simultaneously kissed her.

Tallia put her arms around his neck and sighed her satisfaction into his throat as he wrapped her tightly in his arms and pulled her against him, and his kiss stirred the hot embers of her passion into renewed flame. She felt his hands against her back, pressing her to him, felt his kiss become every moment more passionate as if she were his life support system, and forgot everything except that he seemed to need her as deeply as she needed him. Hungrily she pressed against him, wrapped her arms around his head, opened her mouth for the invasion of his tongue, cried her desire deep in her throat, felt him tremble as he drank it in.

Brad lost his balance and stumbled backwards, and as he found his balance they came to for a brief moment. The sun was disappearing into the ocean, dying in a golden glory that painted the world with richness. It melted over the iron balcony, gilded the plants, glistered from the ice in his abandoned glass, and two ice cubes that sat where they had spilled onto the chaise longue. He felt like Midas, with everything he looked at turning to gold. He looked down at the woman beside him. Her hair, her skin, her eyes all glowed. She, too, was gold, but gold that was warm and melting under his touch. Without a word, he bent and lifted her into his arms, and as he moved towards the bedroom his mouth found hers again.

Later, a long time later, arching and trembling under the touch of his body, she whispered, "I love you!" softly, so softly that he thought she did not mean him to hear. It was as if he eavesdropped as she told her secret to God.

That was too much for him, and with a cry he gave himself up to pleasure, passion, and the unbearable sweetness of her embrace.

14

Tallia reached up to drag the phone from its hook and muttered sleepily into what she hoped was the mouthpiece.

"You ran out on me," Brad's voice said softly into her ear, and abruptly she was wide awake. She struggled to sit up, because she needed to have her wits about her.

Last night she had lain listening to Brad's breathing as he slipped into deep sleep. She'd had to force herself to stay awake, because between exhaustion and pure physical satisfaction she had felt drugged. When she was sure he was sleeping soundly, she gently disentangled herself from his embrace, then froze for a moment as he stirred and his hold tightened.

"Mmm?" he muttered.

"Ah have to pee," she whispered faintly, and his hand relaxed. She slipped out of the bed and then stood quietly in the darkness until his breathing found its steady sleep rhythm again. Then she picked up her scattered clothing and moved out into the sitting room, closing the bedroom door behind her. She dressed in darkness, with the help of the moon that now drifted in the black sky, and, finding her handbag, summoned the private elevator. There must be stairs, but she did not know where, and she could only pray that the hum of the motors would not disturb him. Downstairs, without surprise, the doorman had called her a cab.

"'My lord, it is but quid pro quo,'" she recited gently now.

There was a short silence. "Howzzat again?"

She gurgled into laughter. "That's the Shakespeare for *tit for tat*," she explained.

"Right," said Brad. "And what's your excuse?"

"Ah had an emergency call very early and didn't want to wake y'all, of course," she recited.

"Is that word for word?" he asked dryly, recognizing his own lie in her mouth.

"Ah'm what they call a quick study."

"That means you memorize all the stupid things people say and use it on them when the occasion arises?"

She laughed, glad to find him so quick. "Something like that."

"Am I going to see you tonight?" he said, changing the angle of attack.

Tallia suddenly felt rushed, as if she had no time to catch her breath. "Oh, Brad," she protested.

"Natasha, don't tell me you don't want to see me again," he commanded, in a tone that meant he would not believe her.

"I won't tell you that, Brad, but I have other things to do."

"Like what?" he demanded, and she smiled secretly at the sound of jealousy in his voice. One way or the other, maybe Brad would fall harder than he figured he was going to. She made a quick decision that jealousy might be her friend in this.

"Ah do have other friends, Brad."

"Male friends?"

She didn't answer that, and he quickly followed it up with, "Why do you want to see other men?"

At that, she had to laugh. "Brad, do you or do you not see other women?"

"No!"

Her heart sank in her breast. "So if Ah told you that that scientist mentioned that she went to your cottage with you yesterday, that would be a lie?"

There was silence for the space of a long breath. "Ah, yes, that had slipped my mind," he said ruefully.

"Are you going to go on seeing her?"

"Natasha, I cannot tell a lie. I am."

"For how long?"

"Impossible to say."

"Brad, if you had to choose between us, right now, which would you choose?"

He heaved a sigh. "At this point in time, I have to admit I would not be able to make a choice between you."

Tallia just didn't know whether to laugh or cry. "Well, then, y'all won't mind checking her availability this evening, will you?" she said.

"Look, Natasha, there's something I want to explain to you tonight. And someone I want you to meet. Please. Couldn't you—?"

She really was not proof against him if he was going to plead like that.

"Oh, Brad, Ah guess so!"

"Seven?" he said, keeping the triumph from his voice.

"Hello?"

"Is that Tallia?"

There was a quick, suspicious pause. "Who's speaking, please?"

"This is Brad."

"Oh, Brad! Hi, how are you?"

"Who were you afraid it was?"

"Oh, just somebody I don't want to talk to. You know."

"Henry Clubbins?"

"Henr—? Oh, no! Are you kidding? Henry hasn't tried to call since I left. Congratulations, your team won. Or did I say that already?"

He frowned. "Did you watch yesterday's game?"

"Yeah, with my—" She broke off, and he pursued it.

"With your?"

She laughed. "What a game! What a touchdown! Did you see that run?"

He couldn't help joining in her enthusiasm. It had been a great game. "I did."

"So, what's up?"

"Tallia, I'd like to see you for dinner tonight. Are you free?"

She made a little noise of pleasure in her throat. "Really? Okay, yeah, that would be great!"

Brad paused. "You're sure?"

"Yeah, why?"

He coughed. "There's someone I'd very much like you to meet."

"Okay, sure. Who is it?"

"A very good friend who I'm sure you'll like."

"That's fine."

"Seven?" said Brad.

"You did *what?*" Tallia demanded in stunned amazement. "Bel, how *could* you?"

"Well, come on, who was I supposed to be if not you, answering your phone at eight in the morning?" Bel demanded indignantly. "You don't want him to think you're gay, do you?"

"You could have said I had to think it over!"

"Yeah, or I could have said no! I didn't know what to do and I had to make a choice, Tallia!"

Tallia leapt out of bed and strode excitedly into the sitting room. "My God, Bel, what am I going to do? Omigod, omigod! This is terrible!"

Bel, trailing after her, stared at her sister with a wild surmise. "Tal, for goodness' sake, what's the problem? I thought you were dying to see him!"

Tallia whirled and flung out her arms dramatically. "*Natasha* just accepted a date with Brad tonight!"

Bel sat down as her knees folded under her. "Oh. Oh boy. Oh boy oh boy oh boy. Sorry, sis, and here I thought I was being so quick! Boy, am I stupid! I didn't even think—wait a minute, though, Tal! Wait just a minute! Why—"

"*Why does Brad want a date with both of me tonight?*" Tal asked right along with her, and the two girls gazed wide-eyed at each other for a long, long moment, their eyes and mouths slowly going wider and wider.

"He told me there was—"

"*Someone special he wanted you to meet?*" Tal screeched. And when Bel nodded, she demanded, "What kind of game is he playing at? Why does he want us to meet, and on the same date?"

"Maybe he hopes you'll be friends."

"Just name me one guy who wanted his different girl-friends to be friends with each other."

"Mohammad. I read that. He wanted all his wives to get along."

Tallia glared at her. "Get real! Mohammad was a prophet. Ordinary men don't want women talking behind their backs, comparing notes."

"Well, there's only one way to find out."

Tal went still. "Only..." She heaved a deep breath. "Are you thinking what I'm thinking?"

"I guess I am," Bel said, then blew out expressively and shook her head. "But I'm also wondering how this is going to end." Then she answered her own question. "I guess, the way Mom always used to say whenever we were playing our games. 'This will only end in tears, girls.'"

"I knew this would end badly," Jake said.

"What do you mean? It hasn't even begun to end yet, let alone badly."

"Yes, it has, Brad," said his friend. They were eating lunch in the Fitness Now restaurant. It wasn't a venue they often frequented, but today Brad had insisted. "It has ended with you out of your tiny mind, just the way I always said it would. Are you *crazy*, what you're telling me?"

"What's crazy about it? Lots of people do it. Mohammad had ten wives or something."

"Well, then, Mohammad had one heck of a lot of trouble in his home life!" Jake informed him. "Take it from me!"

Brad scratched his ear. "Actually, I think you're right. They used to go into cabals against each other, telling him he always smelled of garlic when he left wife number three's house and things like that."

"Really? How'd you find out a thing like that?"

"By reading a little further than the Business Section, Jake."

"Well, anyway, it only goes to prove my point."

"Mohammad had ten. I'm only proposing to have two."

"Mohammad, as I understand it, was a prophet. You're merely human. You'll get your eyes scratched out even suggesting it. Worse." He shuddered, just thinking about the possibilities. "I don't understand why you don't just—"

"I don't think so," Brad was saying.

"What are you going to suggest? That you all three share your place? 'It's so roomy we could each have a separate bedroom and still have space to swing the cat'?"

"I'll see what suggestions Tallia and/or Natasha come up with."

"Do they know yet that you hope to feed them simultaneously tonight?"

Brad smiled. "Oh, I think they probably do. They are on what you might call speaking terms, don't forget."

"Which is more than either will be with you, when the cat is out of the bag."

"Jake, what is this cat you keep talking about? I don't have a cat."

"Well, my advice to you is to get one, because after this little episode you won't be much use to women."

"Care to take a small bet on that?"

"You telling me neither of them has cancelled tonight?"

"Not so far. I've been checking my voice mail."

Jake shook his head, and then eyed his friend seriously. "You're sure this is the way to handle it? You're absolutely sure you're not going to lose everything? Women resent these kinds of head games, you know.

You might not be able to come back from a stand like this. What if you can't convince—''

He broke off as there was a cry behind him. ''Brad! Hi! I didn't know you ever ate here!'' and turned to see Tallia Venables coming up to their table.

''Hi, Tallia. You remember Jake.''

''Yeah, hi, Jake.''

''Tallia.''

''Will you join us, Tallia? We're waiting for coffee, but—''

She smiled. ''Do you mind if I don't, Brad? I've got the designer here, and we have things to discuss.''

''No problem.''

''Anyway, I'll be seeing you tonight.'' She smiled and tilted her head. ''Is Natasha Fox the person you want me to meet tonight?''

Brad blinked. ''Yeah, uh, yeah, she is.''

Tallia smiled broadly. ''Yeah, she had a suspicion, she said. I met her in the elevator this morning. See you both tonight, then.''

She waved and moved over to another table, chatted to a waitress, and sat down, as lighthearted as a lark. Brad, a small frown between his eyebrows, gazed at her for a moment.

''Well, well, well!'' Jake's voice burst in on his reverie. ''That's one for the books, isn't it? Weren't you kind of expecting a small women's uprising over this?''

Brad, still frowning, nodded. ''I certainly thought one of them would cancel. I figured it would be Tallia, and then I was going to explain it all to Natasha as the woman of the world and enlist her aid in convincing Tallia it would be a good thing.''

Jake was shaking his head in disbelief. ''Boy, you sure do play with fire.''

"I have to think about what this means."

"That, in fact, is why we are eating here," Jake realized. "To give Tallia an easy opportunity to cancel. 'Oh, Brad, I have to work late!' Am I right?"

But Brad was thinking too hard to hear. He stared across the restaurant at Tallia. "What the heck has she got up her sleeve now?" he demanded, of no one in particular.

"I still think you should let me dress as Tallia, and you go as Natasha."

"Don't be ridiculous!" said Tallia. "Do you think he wouldn't notice?"

"Men never look at me when you're dressed to kill," Bel said sadly. "No reason to think Brad's any different."

"Brad knows me as Tallia. Of course he's going to look at me! I mean you!" Tal said irritably. She didn't like the suggestion that it was Natasha Brad really preferred, though in her heart she was afraid it was true. There was a kind of wildness in him when he made love to Natasha, but he'd been so controlled with Tallia at the lake she wasn't even sure the whole thing couldn't be written down as charity.

"What if he dies of the shock when he sees you?"

"Why should he do that?"

"People have heart attacks, you know."

"Brad's thirty-three, Bel. And I am quite sure he doesn't have a weak heart. Anyway, if he's really planning to suggest a ménage à trois he deserves a bit of a shock," Tallia replied grimly.

Bel shrugged. "You know best," she said, in tones which clearly indicated she did not think so. "So, what are you going to do?"

Tal smiled. "I'm going to dress as myself, and see which one of me he thinks I am. Because whatever one he sees when he looks at the real me, that's the one he likes."

Bel buried her head in her hands. "Amateur psychology, oh boy oh boy! How could I guess that you majored in applied science?"

Two buzzers rang within the space of a minute at Tallia's building that evening. In Tallia's apartment, Bel was stationed. "Hi, Brad," she said in her best Tallia voice. "Be right down."

In Bel's apartment, Tallia answered as Natasha. "Ready, Natasha?" Brad asked, and she sang, "Ah'll be raht there." She buzzed the door open so that he could wait inside.

Instantly she picked up the phone and rang her own number. "Has he rung you?" she demanded when Bel picked up.

"Just now. Are you going down?"

Tallia took a deep breath. "Yup."

"Can I come watch the bloodshed?"

"Bel, will you cut that out? I'm nervous enough as it is!"

"Okay, sorry! Good luck!"

Brad was standing at the lobby windows, looking towards the late sun, but when the elevator doors opened and she stepped out he turned and watched her approach. True to her plan, Tallia smiled a welcome, but said nothing, so that her voice would not give her away.

Brad stared at the woman who approached him. Her long pale blond hair was clean, shining and loosely waving back from her ears and down over her shoulders in a simple style he had never yet seen on her. Her eyes, the colour of the tropical sea now, were lightly made up under high, arching eyebrows that gave her an open, innocent look. Her full, luscious mouth was brushed with a faint glossy pink. Over her perfect body she wore a sweetheart-bodiced, full-skirted cotton dress the same colour as her eyes, with a tiny white bolero that revealed a gold chain at her throat. On her feet, tan-coloured sandals with a small heel. She carried a matching tan leather bag in hands that had short, clear-polished nails. For jewellery she wore pretty scarab earrings and a gold bangle on her delicate wrist. She was perfect. Completely perfect. The woman of his dreams.

He had known it, and yet feared that it could not be so at the same time.

He smiled, moved to meet her, lifted her hand and drew it through his arm. "You are the most staggeringly beautiful woman I have seen in my entire life," he said in a low, almost harsh voice. "But I am not going to kiss you now because I can't risk letting myself start."

She stared up at him. "Who am I, Brad?" she whispered.

He laughed, and, instantly breaking his own rule, bent and kissed her, once, on the mouth. "You," he informed her, "are the eternal Eve. You are the woman of my dreams. Now let's get out of here before that sofa starts to seem like the best idea I've had all day."

"Aren't we going to wait for—?"

He smiled at her quizzically, as if she were being foolish. "For a girl with the best brains of her year, you're being pretty slow," he chided.

He had the pleasure of watching her jaw literally drop. "Brad!" she exclaimed. "You—you *know!*"

He laughed in pure delight. "Of course I know, my

darling. Just how much of a fool do you think one man can be?''

He opened the door and shepherded her out into the late sunshine. "But—when? *When?*" she gasped. "You never gave me a clue!''

Brad bent to open the Porsche, and she had to climb inside. "We have a lot to talk about," he assured her. "But there's plenty of time.''

Brad refused to discuss anything important while he was driving, and so, fretting with impatience, and unable to concentrate on any other subject, Tallia sat and waited through the ten-minute drive. He pulled up and parked outside the first restaurant he had taken her to as Natasha, and later as Tallia.

"Good evening, madam, good evening, Mr. Slinger," said the maitre d' smoothly. "Very nice to see you ag—" He frowned, blinked, and looked at Tallia, then immediately wiped all curiosity from his face and smiled blandly again.

"Thank you," said Tallia, following as he led the way to their table. It was a fashionable, ''in'' place, but with excellent food nevertheless, in which Brad was quite capable of commandeering one of the best tables; but the waiter led them to a table for two, in a quiet nook half-hidden by a screen, that might easily be overlooked by a celebrity-seeking eye, or someone wanting to table-hop with friends.

He sat with his back to the room, with only her to look at. With meticulous precision and patience he ordered a fabulously expensive champagne, and when it came and was poured, he lifted her glass and offered it to her, then lifted his own.

"What are we drinking to?'' she asked.

He smiled. "To a future that I hope will be a little less crazy than the past few weeks has been, but always interesting."

Tallia's heart kicked hard. "All right, I'll drink to that."

They looked into each other's eyes as they smiled and drank, and then Brad set down his glass and quirked an eyebrow at her.

"Tallia, my darling, how long were you going to carry on with your crazy masquerade, and what made you imagine that I could be so blind for so long?"

"It's a long story, Brad," she began softly.

"I'm sure it is, my darling. But I'm sure it will be as entertaining as it is long."

She did want to explain. She didn't know what he might be imagining her reasons were, but probably something a lot worse than the truth. So she embarked on a halting, slightly garbled explanation, beginning with the ad and the responses she had had to it. "And I mean, no one, *no one,* not even a woman—do you know Marielle Humphries, Brad?" she interjected. It was the name of a well-known used car heiress.

"Yes, I know her."

"Well, even she couldn't see anything except that I was attractive. It was just as if blond hair and—and—"

"And physical perfection," he supplied.

"Well, whatever—I might just as well have had a sign tattooed on my forehead, reading DUMB BLONDE. And then Damon wanted me to—" She explained about Damon and her horror when she discovered who his rich old goat was.

Brad grinned. "So that stumble when you met me was authentic?"

"Oh, yes, I was flabbergasted! But still I thought I

had to tell you, but then, in the car you—Brad, you were just so smitten!''

''And how,'' he said in fond memory, smiling at her in a way that made her glad she was already sitting down, because her legs were suddenly rubber.

''And I thought—he can't see past the enhanced bra, how is he ever going to be able to listen to anything I say, and…between me and Bel we kind of cooked up the idea that I'd dress up plain for our meeting a couple of days later.''

''Not plain enough,'' Brad said. ''I wanted Tallia, too, though it took me longer to recognize the feelings.''

''So you were fooled for a while?''

''Oh yes.''

''When did you find out?''

He kept smiling at her in a way that made her bones honey. ''My darling, did you really imagine I could make love to you and not recognize that I had both Tallia and Natasha in my arms?''

Her eyes opened and her jaw went slack. *''Then?''*

He inclined his head and drank more champagne. ''But then—is *that* why you left in the morning and didn't—'' She broke off. ''Brad, were you very angry?''

He set his glass down, and his jaw seemed to tighten with the memory. ''I was pretty angry for the first couple of hours. I went down onto the beach and cursed women and my stupid gullibility for a while.''

''Were you going to stop seeing me?''

''I was going to stop seeing you. Or at least I imagined I was. I wouldn't have been able to stick to the decision, of course.''

''And then what happened?''

''Well, I was sitting on a beached log as the sun came up, swearing at the world, and the, uh—homeless person whose bedroom I had wandered into got up and began commiserating with me.''

She let out a gurgle of laughter. "He did?"

"Yes, and when we had discussed the perfidy of women who will stop at nothing to get what they want, he said something very wise, my darling. In fact, I later discovered that his nickname on the homeless circuit was Wise William."

"And what wise thing did Wise William say?" Tallia said, entering into the spirit of the recital. She drank and opened her eyes at him.

"If you look at me like that, you won't get any dinner," he warned her, so she did it again. Brad reached for her hand and squeezed it hard. "And you won't get this story," he added threateningly.

"Oh!" Tallia tilted her head and put on an I'm-being-a-good-girl expression. "Come on, what did Wise William say?"

"He said, as near as I can remember, 'Correct me if I'm wrong, but there's two women that you can't make up your mind between, and you just found out they're both the same woman, and what you're wondering is, why did she do it?' and I said, 'That's right,' and Wise William said, 'Why do you care why she did it?' and, my darling, I couldn't answer. He was right. The essential thing was that I had found what probably no other man in the world ever had—both halves of his ideal woman in one woman. Why should I be bitter about the how or the why? And I suddenly realized that what was really bothering me was the fear that if it was *all* a hoax, then you might not like me either as Natasha or as Tallia, and until then I'd been pretty sure both of you did like me.''

"I guess I gave myselves away."

He smiled and picked up her hand. "And I realized that what I should be thinking about was how to make you love me. I decided that, whatever your reasons for the double game you were playing, I had one strong card in my hand."

"Which was?"

He smiled that smile again, lifted her hand and kissed the palm, and she shivered as sensation bolted through her.

"That," said Brad in satisfaction. "I thought, at the very least, I can maybe make her physically addicted to me. And maybe love might follow."

"But—you were treating me so badly—telling each of me lies about the other."

"Jealousy has a role, doesn't it? I wanted to see if I could make you jealous, see if either of your disguises gave your real feelings away."

"And I guess both of me did, huh?"

"I wasn't sure till last night."

Suddenly, remembering that whisper, she blushed. She said hastily, "But it wasn't just to make me jealous that you played all those games back at me! You were punishing me, too, admit it!"

He grinned and inclined his head. "I have to say I enjoyed your confusion, after suffering so much confusion at your hands."

"You made me jump through hoops!" she accused, her eyes glinting laughter. "I thought you were the worst playboy the Western world had ever seen!"

"My darling, I do have my own imp, but I hope to keep him under better control in future."

"And what were you going to do tonight? Inviting both of me on the same date!"

"Well, I was pretty sure that only one of you would turn up, unless you decided to draft Bel again."

"You guessed that, huh?"

"It was pretty obvious. But it seemed unlikely that you would risk it at close quarters. So I was going to tell whichever of you showed up that I loved both of you and wanted us all to live together."

Suddenly all the laughter went out of her and she was breathless. "You— Brad, what were you going to say that for?" she whispered.

"Because I mean it." His eyes were dark. "Tallia, will you come and live with me, and be my love?" he asked, as if afraid that she would say no, and that her no would kill him.

"Oh, Brad, oh, Brad, do you really mean that?"

He said roughly, "Damn it, I want to kiss you! What the devil did I bring you to a public place for?"

She was fainting with the sensations that coursed through her at the look that was now naked in his eyes. "Brad, do you—do you love me?"

"Tallia," he said, "you aren't the only one who whispers secrets to the universe. I whispered that secret the first night I made love to you, knowing who you really were, and a very painful secret it was, coming as it did at the moment I discovered you were conning me. Yes, I love you. As Natasha and as Tallia, as a beautiful, intelligent young woman and when you are a beautiful, intelligent old woman. In sickness and in health. Please give me your answer, Tallia."

She smiled her yes. Then her head fell helplessly back on her neck as his kiss scorched her palm.

Epilogue

"Would that be Bel?" said a deep, masculine voice.

"Yeah, it would," Bel said cheerfully.

"Ah...now, how will I put this? Bel, my name is Jake Drummond. I'm a friend of Brad Slinger. I think you know him."

She was instantly guarded. "I've met him a couple of times. I don't think I could say I *know* him."

"Is your sister with him tonight?"

"Which—ah—do you mean...ah—?" Bel ran out of hesitation and simply stopped speaking. She wasn't going to contribute any more to Tallia's mess than she already had. "Yes, I think so. I mean, yes, she left with him about two hours ago."

"And hasn't returned?"

Now she was alarmed for a totally different reason. "Why? Has something happened? What's happened?"

"No, I'm sorry if I've alarmed you, Bel. Nothing's happened as far as I know. I was just wondering if she would come home with my friend's lifeblood on her hands."

"Ohhhhhh," said Bel on a long-drawn-out, comprehending sigh.

"Exactly."

"Brad knows. That's what you're saying, isn't it?"

"Well, that wasn't what I thought I was saying, but you're very quick. Something I should have expected from Tallia's sister, no doubt."

"Look, I'm eaten up with curiosity, too, but honestly, I don't know anything," Bel said suddenly, realizing that Jake Drummond was probably subject to exactly the same feelings.

"They aren't at his place. Do you know where they went for dinner?" he asked, and as if they were both thinking the same thing, she said, "No. But—"

"But that red Porsche is very distinctive. We might look for it. Are you by any chance hungry?"

"I can be ready in fifteen minutes," said Bel.

"I'll meet you in front of your building."

Later, under a velvet sky, Brad took the long way home again, and parked the car by the sea. She kicked her shoes off, and they walked on the beach hand in hand, sometimes in silence, sometimes speaking, at perfect peace.

"Is this where you met Wise William?" she asked once.

"A little further along."

"Do you think he'll be there? I'd like to meet him."

"He doesn't live here anymore. He's working in my human resources department now."

She turned a smiling face up to his. "Really? You gave him a job?"

"Letting his philosophy rot under a log would be a sad loss to the world."

"I guess I have a lot to thank him for, too. You might still be mad, but for him."

"I like to think I would have wised up on my own, eventually."

When the beach ran into rock, they climbed up the steps and onto the sea wall, remembering the first night they had walked here. "Why wouldn't you let me kiss you that night?" he asked. "I was certain you wanted to, but you were so adamant."

She laughed. "Brad, do you have any idea how fierce you looked that night?"

"No. Was that it? Did I frighten you?"

"Well, in a manner of speaking! I was wearing a very heavy wig that night. If you'd started pulling at it—and it wasn't just a wig, it was my disguise."

He laughed, and they walked further. From behind a cloud a golden half moon sailed out, brushing the world with cool fire. From time to time water splashed up from the rocks below.

Tallia stopped, and Brad immediately stopped and turned to her. Her heart pounding with love, she grinned impishly and whispered, "Oh, Brad, Ah sure do wish y'all would kiss me!"

Without a word he swept her into his arms, hard, and ruthlessly took possession of her mouth. One hand slipped up to hold her head, and his kiss became more passionate, deeply intense, as if he could not get enough of her. At last, when she was fainting with the force of passion that roared through her, he lifted his mouth again, but it was only to draw her head back and press his lips to the panicked pulse in her throat.

His body was already ready for hers, urgent with the desire to give her pleasure, and take it from her. His mouth moved up to hers again, and her head reeled and the stars went out.

"Brad," she whispered, almost frightened at the passion that swept between them. "Brad, not here!"

He lifted his head and heaved a breath. "No, not

here,'' he agreed, his breath heaving. "Let's go home, my darling.''

"Yes,'' she said. "Let's go home.''

* * * * *

DIANA PALMER
ANN MAJOR
SUSAN MALLERY

MONTANA MAVERICKS Weddings

RETURN TO WHITEHORN

In **April 1998** get ready to catch the bouquet. Join in the excitement as these bestselling authors lead us down the aisle with three heartwarming tales of love and matrimony in Big Sky country.

A very engaged lady is having second thoughts about her intended; a pregnant librarian is wooed by the town bad boy; a cowgirl meets up with her first love. Which Maverick will be the next one to get hitched?

Available in **April 1998**.

Silhouette's beloved **MONTANA MAVERICKS** returns in Special Edition and Harlequin Historicals starting in February 1998, with brand-new stories from your favorite authors.

Round up these great new stories at your favorite retail outlet.

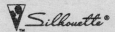

Take 4 bestselling love stories FREE

Plus get a FREE surprise gift!

Special Limited-time Offer

Mail to Silhouette Reader Service™

3010 Walden Avenue
P.O. Box 1867
Buffalo, N.Y. 14269-1867

YES! Please send me 4 free Silhouette Yours Truly™ novels and my free surprise gift. Then send me 4 brand-new novels every other month, which I will receive months before they appear in bookstores. Bill me at the low price of $2.90 each plus 25¢ delivery and applicable sales tax, if any.* That's the complete price and a savings of over 10% off the cover prices—quite a bargain! I understand that accepting the books and gift places me under no obligation ever to buy any books. I can always return a shipment and cancel at any time. Even if I never buy another book from Silhouette, the 4 free books and the surprise gift are mine to keep forever.

201 SEN CF2X

Name	(PLEASE PRINT)	
Address	Apt. No.	
City	State	Zip

This offer is limited to one order per household and not valid to present Silhouette Yours Truly™ subscribers. *Terms and prices are subject to change without notice. Sales tax applicable in N.Y.

BEVERLY BARTON

Continues the twelve-book series— 36 Hours—in April 1998 with Book Ten

NINE MONTHS

Paige Summers couldn't have been more shocked when she learned that the man with whom she had spent one passionate, stormy night was none other than her arrogant new boss! And just because he was the father of her unborn baby didn't give him the right to claim her as his wife. Especially when he wasn't offering the one thing she wanted: his heart.

For Jared and Paige and *all* the residents of Grand Springs, Colorado, the storm-induced blackout was just the beginning of 36 Hours that changed *everything!* You won't want to miss a single book.

Available at your favorite retail outlet.

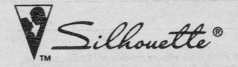

 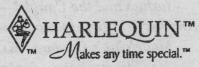